Hello Life

ALSO BY THE AUTHOR:

Thumbelina

Hello Life

a novel

ANDREA KOENIG

Published by
Soho Press, Inc.
853 Broadway
New York, NY 10003

Library of Congress Cataloging-in-Publication Data

Koenig, Andrea.
Hello life / Andrea Koenig.
p. cm.
ISBN 1-56947-391-9
EAN 978-1-56947-391-7
1. Orphans–Fiction. 2. Teenage girls–Fiction. 3. Female
friendship–Fiction. 4. Teenage pregnancy–Fiction. 5.
Cancer–Patients–Fiction. I. Title.

PS3561.03342H45 2005
813'.54–dc22   2004065079

10 9 8 7 6 5 4 3 2 1

Acknowledgments

I am grateful to Elyse Cheney, my literary agent, for her diligent reads of this manuscript. Thanks to all at Soho Press. Scott Williams patiently revealed the mysteries of a salmon hatchery. Robert Michael Pyle's book, *The Butterflies of Cascadia*, was an excellent resource. Thanks to Drs. Eric Sherburn, Ann LaCasce, and Serena Koenig, and Gary Protto, for the notes and comments. Special thanks to Walter Gerard.

I will make nothing better by crying . . .

—Archilochus

One

My mom died on one of the few sunny days we had last August. The reasons were bad luck and the fact that, in a town otherwise going belly up, her beauty shop thrived even on Saturdays. She had appointments up the highway with a couple of loggers' wives and for old customers like them she made house calls. She rolled a perm corkscrew tight for one lady and in the other's drab hair she left thick blonde streaks. Nothing made my mom happier.

The highway that took her back to town was an old two lane that skirted the Columbia. Halfway between the loggers' trailers and the edge of town the river bends sharply and cliffs rise over the road. Water trickles down the black rock, and alder and fir have wedged into its cracks.

My mom had the window down as she drove. She was singing along to the radio. The sign says SLOW, and it shows falling rocks, but my mom only wore her glasses when applying a foil. She sped around the corner into a couple of good-sized chunks of cliff that weren't there when she'd passed a few hours before. Her boyfriend's Corvette flipped and rolled. She never saw the point of a seatbelt and the cops said her pretty, 37-year-old body was thrown from hell to breakfast down the narrow highway.

She was the third bad accident in as many years on that spot, with the Columbia, our town's namesake, spread out like a parking lot twenty feet below. The others were loggers, though, driving into town in full-size V-8's to buy groceries and stop at Miz Hundy's tavern, and they got off with a broken collarbone and banged-up face.

I work for Miz Hundy, and she said a sixteen-year-old girl was in no position to handle funeral arrangements. She was a plain woman with tough, large hands and a face lined unfairly by wind and cigarettes. Nothing about Miz Hundy seemed inclined toward money. She had plenty, though. She and her younger sister, Mrs. Parker, agreed my mom should be cremated. Her ashes could be scattered on the river so she would know the kind of freedom that eluded her in life.

I said my mother was going to be buried with a headstone. She was going to get the same treatment every other dead person got. I said this for three days straight and I suppose this is how I survived early on, by arguing against formidable Miz Hundy, the richest woman in town, and her Catholic younger sister, neither one a fan of my mom's. What I told them was I didn't care how many people in town disliked her, we weren't throwing her on the river.

"Spreading," Mrs. Parker corrected, pursing her little pink mouth and batting at her sister's cigarette smoke with her tiny, fat hand. Ornate Suffering Jesus hung down her large chest. "Scattering, even. Nobody suggested your mother was a softball, dear."

I love silver, normally, but I'm no fan of wearing a cross, when just getting up in the morning is enough weight for anyone to carry.

We were sitting in Miz Hundy's cramped kitchen above her tavern. I'd been sleeping on her couch in the next room since it happened. My cat Lou and me. The close quarters on top of everything else had my nerves in pieces.

"You don't want L.D. to have a stone to cry over, Mrs. Parker," I replied, "because you used to be married to him."

"I believe he mourns his Corvette," Mrs. Parker said, "I'll give you that."

"Nona, really!" Miz Hundy paused with the hot kettle in her hand and regarded her younger sister with her pale, nearly colorless eyes. "You're not *still* carrying a torch for that man?"

Mrs. Parker and L.D. divorced years ago. Some people said it was because they couldn't have children. My mom said no, they broke up over matters of temperament.

"You're too close to this kid, I've said it before." Mrs. Parker continued fluttering the air with her plump, ineffective hand.

A lot more than ten years separated them. They had nothing sisterly about them at all. One was short and wide as the river, the other tall and bony. One cleaned houses, the other owned real estate, quite a bit of it on this very street where we sat, Ninth Street, including the building just a few down where my mom and I had lived. People said Miz Hundy's show barn, where I worked, drained her pockets and her tavern filled them right back up without her noticing.

Miz Hundy was old, she'd seen it all, said the expression on her face. "If we give your mother a gravestone, Gwen, I don't want you up there. It's one thing if L.D. wants to moon around after her memory, but I have better things in mind for you." She gave me a stern look. "If you can agree to be sensible about this, we'll bury her."

She forbade me, however, to view my mother's body.

Two

My father was absent from the church service. My birth sixteen years ago drove him out of town and he hadn't cropped up since. All we had left of him was his old friend, Edgar Fuentes, who must have spent the night before the funeral at the sink because he had cleaned every bit of motor oil from under his fingernails. He pulled me into his arms in the rear of church and pressed his face against mine. He smelled like the soap in the gas station toilet. I shoved him away. People were watching, but he was persistent. He slid into the end of my pew, with only Miz Hundy and her sister holding her Rosary between us. During the Act of Contrition I felt him lean and look at me, but I just acted as if he was the one dead.

Afterward we all got in our cars and drove out of town, past the barn where I work and right over the spot where my mom Althea left this earth, literally. The whole long line of us downshifted and nearly stopped to make the sharp turn up the dirt road to the top of the cliff. From where I stood the river was like a cold blue lake, our newsprint mill and the town that's scattered around it hidden behind brush and trees—and the river's decision, millions of years ago, to bend north one final time at this point. Oregon lay on the other side, a mile away: soft green hills and railroad tracks. Upriver a few more minutes the tiny town of Cathlamet is perched on a hill with a view to rival this one. Our dead are nicely situated.

The priest spoke prayers into the damp air and tears rolled down the faces of the loggers' wives. They wore black sweaters, one with black slacks, the other with a polka-dot skirt that blew around her legs. Their hair looked great. I couldn't cry. The air was moist, rain waited in the wings, but I was dry. I hadn't seen evidence of my mom's death. Her death felt like a story, like my father's absence from my life was a story. She was floating out there in the world like Gustavo Pérez. She could reappear any time.

Miz Hundy had closed her tavern for the afternoon and laid out a buffet. She gave her sister her keys and told her to go act hostess till we got there. She'd wait with me for the men to come with the machine. I wanted to see them lower my mother into her hole.

Miz Hundy was on the phone with her bartender, telling him to be sure to set out enough plastic cups. I found a stone bench off by itself behind a huge blackberry bush. I wanted to remember this day, every bit of it, the ladies from the trailers wiping their faces again and again, the priest who said death was nothing but a new beginning, my mother's shiny brass nameplate on her coffin with her whole life held between those two dates: 1963-2000. They'd dressed her in her light denim summer dress, which I thought was a bad idea, but no one listened to me, and put makeup on her (Miz Hundy assured me) and combed out her blonde hair. Was the lid heavy or could I walk over there and lift it to make sure the box was lined with satin and her arms were filled with yellow roses?

A throat cleared. I looked up and saw my father's friend, Edgar Fuentes, hesitating on the dirt path. He had a habit of appearing from thin air.

"So? Now you don't speak to me?"

His long black hair made him look even shorter than he was. He used to let my mom trim it because she had a way of bringing out the Mexican curl. I think she just liked to get her hands in his hair. When he first came back to town, and this was a couple of years ago, she wanted to cut it all off, clean up his look, she told him. "She wants to Samson-me," he used to chuckle to me privately. The suit he'd borrowed was soft charcoal gray, too short and tight in the arms. He had powerful shoulders from all the evenings swimming in our high school pool and very white teeth. "I told you, Edgar, I can't talk to you anymore." I scraped the heel of my pump along the grass underneath the bench.

"You break my heart, kid." He reached into his pants pocket and pulled out a green knit hat. He pulled it down tight on his head. The hat was misshapen and ugly, the first and last thing I ever knitted.

"Don't wear that."

"The last time I looked this was a free country. I can wear my present if I feel like it."

I turned and watched my boss swing up the path toward us in her long black skirt and black shawl.

"Go on, you. Shoo." Miz Hundy made a sweeping motion at the man with her hands.

Edgar gave her a mournful look, held his ground a few seconds, lifted and dropped his shoulders and ambled up the path. "To be continued" hung in the air.

"I'm going to say this quick and get it over with, Gwen." She took cigarettes from the folds of her skirt and jammed one in her mouth. "My sister doesn't think it's right, you living with me. Over a tavern is her main objection, although she has others. If you know anything about me, you know I don't pay attention to what Nona says, but in this case, she's right. I'm a bad influence on you. My friends, the company I keep, all that."

"Can I have one of those, Miz Hundy?"

The woman hesitated. "This is exactly what Nona means. How I'd aid and abet you straight into trouble. More trouble." She handed me the pack. "The point is, she wants you to live with her. Personally, I think you look too much like your mother to be under Nona's nose day in, day out. You know my sister, though, always willing to pull on a hair shirt at the drop of a hat. She's going to attempt to reform you."

"Is that what she's doing to Lila Abernathy?" I took my smoke and turned away, naming the foster teenager who had been under Nona Parker's roof for two or three weeks already. A junior like me, with a mother often gossiped about (like mine), Lila was recovering from leukemia. She had never been my friend and certainly wouldn't be now.

"Lila Abernathy, from what I understand, needs a good home." Miz Hundy shrugged. "Perhaps you girls will get a little bit of 'the wages of sin are death' thrown in with dinner, but Nona's essentially harmless."

She slipped her hand under my arm and pulled me to my feet. She pushed me gently back onto the path, talking all the while.

"I need you back at my barn as soon as you can manage it, Gwen. The horses miss you and I can't abide a dirty establishment."

"I could go out there now." I stopped and turned to face her.

The men hadn't come yet with their machine. My mother's box remained on its platform, a heavy black cloth hiding the hole. I wished people would have stayed to watch them lower her, but they'd all headed off for sliced ham and beer.

"You can't go to the barn today," Miz Hundy was saying. "You have to put in face time. People want to offer their condolences. You've got to let them." She cupped my elbow in her sturdy hand and pulled me along with her as she strode up the path. "Chin up, my dear. You're made of stern stuff. That's why I like you."

Three

The next afternoon I carried two boxes of jeans and flannel shirts down Miz Hundy's inside staircase and set them in the back of her sister's station wagon, next to cleaning supplies and a cloth bag stuffed with rubber gloves. I set my mom's expensive Martin guitar in the middle seat next to the vacuum cleaner. She bought it for herself when she was about my age and gave it to me years ago.

I wrapped my cat Lou in a towel and held him tight as we drove west down Main from Ninth to Gilbert, the houses getting smaller and the yards weedier as we went. Gilbert Street had pickups parked every which way down its entire length, from stop sign to guardrail at the dead end. Mrs. Parker's house was on the high side of the street, yellow, half-way down, the neatest by far.

A girl sat on the front steps with a scarf on her head as

yellow as the house. Lila Abernathy, or Leukemia Girl, as I had decided I would think of her. I looked at her and she looked at me. Mrs. Parker had to say, "Lila, will you bring one of these boxes up?" or she'd probably be sitting there still.

We left everything in the lady's living room. "Unpack after dinner. The world always looks better after a square meal," Mrs. Parker said cheerfully. She used the toe of one sneaker to ease her heel out of the other and pushed her feet into black slippers that sat near the door. Her feet were so fat they rolled right over the embroidered dragons on the sides.

In the kitchen Lila hooked a chair with her foot and sat down on the edge of it as if it would bite, her long legs crossed at the knee. She was slender, blue-eyed (they could turn hard on a dime), a ballerina with promise in our dreary little mill town, popular until last spring, when she came down with what at first everyone thought was the flu. She didn't say a word until Mrs. Parker started cutting carrots.

"You're going to cook those, right, Mrs. Parker? Remember, germs?"

Mrs. Parker clenched her heavy jaw. "You haven't said a proper hello to Gwen."

"Hello," Lila muttered and turned right back to the woman who wore what I understood was her cleaning uniform, a brown tweed skirt and white blouse, folded up her heavy arms. "If I get an infection, I'm screwed." Lila crossed her arms on the brightly flowered tablecloth Mrs. Parker had probably seen in one of the nicer houses she cleaned, up on the bluff on the east side of town, toward Kelso and the big interstate.

"Screwed," Lila repeated, and opened her hand over her

skinny chest. I hadn't seen her catheter yet, which apparently was inserted into a big vein that drained into her heart. I could see what I thought was a bulge under her tight angora sweater, though, and I'd been told to be on good behavior on account of this.

If I was ever going to go soft on the girl, it would be because she had been put together by the Maker, if you believed in that, with exceptional care. When school started in a few days she would be one of the prettiest juniors, or she would be if she had hair, right up there with her old friend Connie Beller. Connie was soft, though, while Lila had the kind of looks that could cut you. Maybe that had something to do with how quickly her friends dropped her when sickness called her name.

"You must have really got on your mother's nerves down in Portland, Lila," I said, "if she's sent you back here."

"I only see my doctor on an outpatient basis now." Lila shrugged. "I want to graduate from my own high school, if that's OK with you."

"Good luck."

"What's that supposed to mean?"

"Clawing your way back. You should have started over in the big city. And now you're in foster care, which won't exactly help your cause."

"Gwen." Mrs. Parker wagged her head. "Don't."

For the first time since entering the kitchen Lila really looked at me, at my lap more specifically, where fat Lou was slowly calming down from the ride in Mrs. Parker's station wagon. A shelter cat, his nerves were fragile to begin with, and two years of my mom and me yelling at each other over and around him hadn't done him any good. Big tears rolled down his nose. I knew it was the upper-respiratory infection rearing its head but I felt annoyed and guiltier than ever, since I hadn't leaked a drop. I tried to wipe the guy's eye, but he jerked his head away.

"She can't keep that cat, Mrs. Parker. They carry germs."

"I heard your mom won't give you back your car, Lila," I continued. "Isn't that just like her? Didn't your dad give you that car? Not that we should mention *him*. You see that blue Chevy out front? It belongs to *me*. I'm not driving you around. Let's get that straight right now."

"Your mother's truck? You're driving your mother's truck?"

"Why shouldn't I?" I said.

"If it would have started that morning she might still be alive," the girl replied.

"Don't listen to everything people say, Lila." Mrs. Parker frowned.

"The battery in the truck was dead, Ma'am," Lila insisted. "That truck would *not* have rolled down the highway from a few stupid rocks."

"The Lord guides each of us according to His will. We have a new battery now, everything's fine," Mrs. Parker said brightly, flicking a carrot peel off her arm, into the sink. "Gwen, before I forget?" She was speaking quickly, moving us right off the subject of my mother. She went to the fridge to put the half head of cabbage away. "Stay away from that man in the pink house across the street."

Lila rolled her eyes. "A doctor lives there. Dr. Kazlowski. Has the little yellow Volkswagen? I don't think it runs. I've seen him coming and going on his bike. He drinks. Tell her, Mrs. Parker. You know you're dying to."

Nona Parker opened her mouth as if to answer, but changed her mind. She had dark red hair threaded with gray and she patted at her curled bangs, pushing them out of her face.

"You might wonder why I've got girls in my house, not boys," she said, bending over to unload glasses from the dishwasher. "I only take girls. This world is unkind to the female. I'm going to protect you two. One day you'll thank me."

"We have to walk to school, you know. I hope you have better shoes, Lila." I nodded at the green pump hanging off the girl's narrow foot, the leather cracked around the toes.

She screwed up her blue eyes. "At least I don't have horse shit on them."

"You can argue but I forbid swearing." Mrs. Parker pulled her coppery head out of the pot of carrots. "As I was saying. You're attractive girls. I don't want you talking to that doctor. Even saying hello."

"Because he drinks? So do half the people in this town," Lila muttered. "Lucky for your sister, huh, Mrs. Parker? I can't believe I'm back here."

"You're back because Providence has given you a second wind. Let your mother gallivant around Portland. I agree wholeheartedly. Your junior year is no time to enter a big city high school. You're small town girls, both of you, and that's nothing to be ashamed of. A couple of weeks ago I watched that man sit in his front yard all day and pour beer down his gullet," Mrs. Parker continued. "In his lawn chair in the rain. And the way he goes through women? A different one every weekend. And that music he plays. It makes me uncomfortable, I don't mind saying. You can't understand the words and it puts me in a sad frame of mind."

"Speaking of music, I see you've brought a guitar." Lila cocked an eyebrow at me. "I can't have any noise when I'm practicing. I'm a dancer." She cupped her face with her slender hands and stared at me across the fern centerpiece. "Understand?"

I looked away. Something about the way she was trying to provoke me in this moment made me think of my mom.

"I have to practice too, Lila. Every day I practice."

"Oh? What are your professional objectives? Do you plan to do anything with your music?"

"I'm going to use it to tune you out."

"Girls." Mrs. Parker shook her head.

Four

Lila and I were given white bunk beds that were separated but could fit together if a third girl should join us. Not likely, but just in case, we were told. I got the bed under the window and my first night there I leaned on the sill and watched the street slowly darken. I didn't see other kids, just men coming and going in pickups and the silent pink house across the street with weeds in the yard and empty flower boxes I'd been warned to stay away from.

"What's your cat's name?" Lila said finally.

I'd changed into my T-shirt and sweats for bed, but she still wore her tight black angora sweater and black pleated skirt. She'd been pretty much ignoring me for about an hour, sewing ribbon on her pointe shoes. Now she put her thread in the nightstand drawer and said, "Can I hold him? Your cat?"

"He's shy, Lila."

Before Lou could jump off the bed, she got up and slammed her arms around his fat white body. She was probably going to use a grip like that to climb the ladder back to popularity this year.

"All right then, hold him, I'll get his stuff in the car."

I shivered going down the front steps. September had opened chilly. Like Mrs. Parker said, she and her sister had put a new Sears battery in the blue Chevy and towed it here from L.D.'s house up on Fifth, across Main. They didn't know my mom kept her spare key under the floor mat. The Chevy was parked at the curb now, its front fender hanging, a horseless rider, if I could go that far. The streetlight picked out masking tape on the cracked vinyl seat and the steering wheel covered with my mother's fingerprints. I had the eerie thought that if I stared hard enough I could conjure her up behind the wheel. Why not? Had anyone shown me her body? I was supposed to be protected from all that. I could see her sitting there, how she'd jerk down the rearview and pat and pinch the delicate skin at the corners of her eyes. She was forever trying to wake up the deep layer of her skin that had rolled over and surrendered the battle against time.

I dropped the jug of litter on our bedroom floor and asked Lila, "Where's Lou?"

Lila picked up several jars off her nightstand and what looked like a syringe wrapped in plastic and stepped around me. "I told you cats carry germs. I put him out."

"What the fuck?"

"On the back porch." She slammed the bathroom door.

I ran through the kitchen and banged out to the covered back porch. I found nothing behind the washer and dryer and I ran down the steps into Mrs. Parker's backyard. I beat my hands through tall grass and called out to him, come on Lou, come on, and waited perfectly still to hear his reply, but he was gone.

Five

Death in the family or not I had to go to school. Instead of a quick six blocks from Ninth Street to Fifteenth, high school was over a mile away now. The low brick buildings of Columbia High were squeezed in between Dairy Queen, a gas station and several houses with missing porch steps and gable boards torn loose by some winter storm and left gaping. Everyone had complained for years about the lack of parking lots at the high school. Teachers hardly had room for their old cars. Most of us kids had at least a borrowed car from Mom or Dad to drive to our after school jobs, but we clogged up Fifteenth and Main so badly there was a rule against it now. If you were too good for the bus, you walked.

I had a long-legged stride and good work boots. A mile was nothing to me. Lila piddled along behind me in her heels. My chemistry book clearly described particles of opposite charge. That was us, all right.

The gas station where Edgar Fuentes worked and parked his van was right down the street from school. I had to pass the man twice a day. In gray overalls he'd be filling a tank in Full Serve or pushing a credit card through some mini-van's window, his black hair gathered in a rubber band. When he saw me his long face would turn even graver and he'd nod, but I think our conversation at the cemetery got through to him. He never called out. I never paused.

Edgar returned to town two summers ago. After he arrived my mom and I started bickering and never stopped. She was nineteen when she first saw the two of them, Edgar and Gustavo Pérez, my father, standing shoul-der to shoulder inside the door of Miz Hundy's tavern— two Mexicans from Texas who liked beer, blondes and country music. My mother finished her set and went to the bar and pretty soon she had company. They were on their way to Alaska, the men told her, but the water pump in Edgar's van had broken out on the interstate.

"I've changed my mind," the smaller of the two said. Gustavo was carefully dressed in a straw hat and blue, open necked shirt that showed plenty of his dark, thin chest. "I'm not going to freeze my *cojones* off in the North," he said and lifted a strand of my mother's blonde hair that had fallen into her drink and pushed it behind her ear. He smiled into her striking blue eyes. "I like this town fine."

"I'm going to Nashville," my mother replied. "It's all sort-ed out. I leave in a few weeks."

A few weeks came and went. By August she was preg-nant and Gustavo stayed until I was born the following May. He lifted me from my crib, high over his curly head, clucking and cooing. My mother leaned in their bedroom doorway and watched. "Easy come easy go, they say. Well, I want you to know I know you're going, Gustavo."

He held me close to his heart with its strange yearnings to be unrooted and free. "You will not regret my absence, Althea."

"You're never coming back? Not even for her?"

He left without his slow-moving, handsome friend. Months in our wet town, near our big, clear river, began to cool Edgar's memories of the blistering Texas sun. He seemed in no hurry to leave. When he finally did, when I was in elementary school, he went to California, not Alaska. He sent my mother a postcard of the setting sun, purple on the Pacific Ocean, and wrote across the back that roofing houses was a bitch and he missed our town. "Do you think he means he misses you?" I said. "One Mexican will last me a lifetime, thanks," my mom replied. Now Edgar was back, nearly forty, still single, still living on wheels. My mother loudly proclaimed he wasn't welcome, then turned around and invited him to dinner. Shooed her last customer out the door and spent thirty minutes in the bathroom with her curling iron and blue eye shadow, which shoes should I wear with this skirt, honey?

I walked past Edgar's gas station and, six blocks down Main, turned up our old street and climbed our back stairs to see if Lou was curled in a white ball on our landing. I did this every afternoon, lingering for an hour or so. If the cat dish was empty, I'd unlock our door for the bag of food on the counter. It was like the people who lived here had left on vacation. Any day they'd be back to put bread in the toaster and dishes in the dish rack and their elbows on the round table wedged against the fridge and the wall.

When we had company we'd take off the legs and roll it into the living room. One of the three chairs was slightly turned as if someone had gotten up quickly and left the room. Maybe my mother's ghost.

When I asked Miz Hundy she admitted, yes, she'd been approached about the building, the beauty shop especially. Lonna Caruthers, who ran a dingy salon above the Laundromat, wanted to assume my mother's lease. "Wants my mom's customers, you mean," I muttered. Miz Hundy said she didn't know what she was going to do with the building yet, but she was a businesswoman, she would have to do something. The very next Saturday I packed my mother's things. I did this slowly and stopped often to see if I felt her presence in the little shop downstairs with her red swivel chair. "You'll never believe who wants this place, Mom," I prayed while I dropped her pens and appointment book into a cardboard box. I tried to pass that message out into the air. Did I hear a reply? "That goddamn excuse for a redhead will never keep my customers." Did I hear that? Or was I making it up? I reached into the box and opened the spiral book to the Saturday she died. The page was blank, as I'd known it would be. She never recorded her visits to the trailers. They were her old friends, those ladies up the highway, and she liked to keep things informal with them, which is exactly how they paid her. In dribs and drabs.

Into the box went her three pair of good scissors, her heavy pink hair dryer she'd used for years, her narrow white sneakers she sometimes changed into during the afternoon if her calves ached, the picture of me when I was little and didn't cause her any trouble. She kept a mini-fridge behind her counter for cold drinks and I peeled off her red chili pepper magnet from Santa Fe and the one from Jackson Hole with cowboys sitting on a split rail fence that said 14 BUN SALUTE! Lynn Beller gave them to her since my mom never traveled. Other customers had started the habit, and she had a magnet from Niagara Falls and from Las Vegas, a showgirl hiding behind a feather fan. I saved them all.

The inventory I left on the shelves for Miz Hundy to deal with: finishing paste, every kind of conditioner under the sun, mousse, shampoo. One-third of my mom's business came from selling this stuff to her customers for way inflated prices. She put that money in the bank. Buying this shop and our apartment upstairs had been her dream for as long as I could remember. They had that in common, my mother and Miz Hundy—they both ran successful businesses in a town that otherwise was pretty sad. The loggers kept to their trailers up the highway unless they needed groceries or Miz Hundy's rowdy tavern. The trees they cut and yarded out of the woods sailed raw from our export dock to Japan. The people in that country preferred to saw their lumber themselves. As far as our mill went, only one of the big rolls of newsprint was in operation anymore. You couldn't blame all this on the new Wal-Mart they'd built out by the interstate. Everyone but my mother and Miz Hundy and her sister seemed to cross the river and work in Portland these days. They did their shopping down there while they were at it. Our old bank, the little paint store, the secondhand furniture store, all had FOR RENT in their windows.

Sometimes I'd joke to my mom that I should go into business with her. She had so many customers this last summer, I'd have to put down my guitar most afternoons and come downstairs to roll a perm or trim some kid while she handled a regular who'd dropped in without an appointment. (They tipped well, those ladies.)

"I built this business," was her reply. "You go build your own thing."

"You did not, you inherited it."

"From who? Old Mrs. Tooney? That lady was nearly blind when I started working for her. I'm the best thing that ever happened to her."

We had this conversation, argument, whatever you call it, a lot lately. And another one that went something like this:

"If I leave town to become famous will you come with me, Mom?" On this particular occasion I was at the kitchen counter making tuna sandwiches. She'd been down in her shop all day. She sat in her chair with her head back, a beer in her hand.

"Oh, Gwen, for Pete's sake. Nobody on their way to stardom takes their mother."

"You used to sing with your mother."

"Locally, but I had no intention of taking her to Nashville. Not so much mayo. I'll take mine dry."

I scowled. "You never even made it onto the bus."

"I met Gustavo Pérez, as you well know. Don't look at me like that with his goddamn eyes, either."

I slid her sandwich across the table. "One day you're going to tell me everything about him. More than that I have his eyes."

This was weeks, probably a whole month, before she died. She shook her thick blonde hair out of her face (eighteen years since she'd caught my father's eye and still no gray) and pulled her cigs from the back pocket of her loose cotton pajama pants. They had blue flowers all over them and she changed into them the minute she finished work, always.

"On the one hand I'd tell you to stay away from boys, but you already go so far out of your way not to act like me, I don't think you're going to have to deal with getting pregnant before your time."

"You said deep down you knew what you were doing."

"I was nineteen. What do you want me to say? My only good quality is that I'm honest. I am, at least with you. I don't want you to turn out like me."

I left the box on the shop counter and climbed our back stairs. We used to leave the door at the top open so we could steal Miz Hundy's heat in winter and so my mom could yell stuff up at me. What to make for dinner, was I doing my homework, could I put such and such record on the stereo, loud please, could I come down and sweep up hair?

At the top was our living room. The curtains were closed, the room felt heavy with emptiness. Her pink sweater was thrown over the back of our green velour couch. She'd forgotten it that Saturday. I knew in the bathroom her hair dryer would be plugged into the wall, a smaller model than the one she used downstairs, her mascara fallen into the sink. I had touched nothing. She had stepped out for a second, she'd be right back. Two weeks had passed with the apartment waiting like this. I couldn't step into it. I stayed on the edge, my heels on the top stair, until finally I turned and left.

Six

The rules at Mrs. Parker's house were simple. Lila and I had to clear the dinner table and do the dishes. We were supposed to keep up our room and make sure our dirty clothes landed in the hamper in the corner of the bathroom and not on the floor of our closet. We couldn't swear or have boys over. She gave us each a little cross on a silver chain. Lila wore hers. I put mine in the dresser drawer.

My third or fourth night there I cleared the table and went down to the bedroom and took out my guitar. The D-2 model was the biggest, loudest guitar Martin made, but its tone could also be mellow and undeniably soothing. My mind calmed.

"Yoo hoo?" Lila appeared in the doorway with a dish towel in her hand. "You've demonstrated you can hit the high notes, now shut up, will you? I have to practice."

It was impossible to think about my mom, about anything, with this girl around.

"You have a hearing problem?" she demanded.

"Cigarette?" I leaned over my guitar for my suede coat at the foot of my bed.

"I don't smoke," Lila said. "I'm in my first remission from cancer of the blood. I hope it lasts forever, but you should never get your hopes up. It's not polite to offer me a cancer stick."

"Say a Hail Mary for my sorry ass." I shrugged. "I just live here temporarily. I don't share Mrs. Parker's religion."

She fingered the knot in her yellow scarf. "Play something cheerful," Lila ordered, and she sat down on her pink quilt drawn tight over her mattress. Stuffed animals lined her wall. I'd have to bring my pillow over from our apartment and my eiderdown with cows and pigs I'd had forever. Get rid of this blue bedspread some other kid had used before me.

"I'll play Hank Williams' one and only happy song if you pray me through my geometry test this Friday, Lila." I tightened the high E.

"I told you, I don't pray."

"Oh, come on. You put that necklace on in a hurry."

She didn't answer. I came at her from another angle. "Dennis Bly sits behind me."

"Whoop de do," Lila replied.

I and everybody at Columbia High knew Lila had asked the lanky cross-country runner to a dance last October, nearly a year ago now, the one where girls had to ask guys. He'd said yes, but immediately after the event had asked Connie Beller, Lila's rival, to be his girlfriend. They'd been inseparable ever since, those two. Dennis was from the wrong side of the tracks and Connie the right. Although I had no ambition to do it myself, I admired someone who could pull himself up by his bootstraps.

"Dennis didn't say a word today," I continued, "the whole class. Except to tell those guys in back a dirty joke. Forget the prayer. From you of all people. Geometry's easy."

"You should have taken it when you were a sophomore."

"You were pretty good friends with him once, Lila."

"What was the joke?"

"How a leather wallet turns into a suitcase when you stroke it."

Lila slipped off her heels and flexed and arched her long, ugly feet, the joke going right over her head. She pulled her toe shoes off the closet door knob.

"I can't stand my mom right now," she said, knotting the satin ribbon at her bony ankle. "And vice versa. It's been a lot of pressure on us, living together for so many months, while my life hung in the balance. She has this new job. She needs her space right now, but she didn't drive recklessly down the highway like some people we know, she just told me to move out."

Her foot didn't make it to the level of her ear. I grabbed a handful of her leotard and shoved her into the closet. She fell easily and with little noise. She was breath on a window. I could have erased her with my hand.

"What'd you do that for?" she gasped, her hand opening over her heart.

I brushed off my hands. The bedroom door didn't open. "You know like everyone knows it was an accident, Lila."

"She was going too fast around that corner—"

I raised my hand to hit her. My chest rattled. I felt ready to cram any ugly words back down the girl's throat.

Lila crawled across the floor and huddled on her bed, gathering her long legs into her arms.

"Even Mrs. Parker won't be able to do much with you," she murmured. And got up abruptly. Minced her way over to the dressing table near the door, ignoring me now.

Both the table and matching chair were antiques with curved cherry wood legs on loan from Miz Hundy. Her tiny apartment was packed with stuff like this. We were supposed to use the table to apply makeup and fix our hair— share it, in other words, but Lila had plunked down her large glass case that held her butterfly collection.

She knelt and pulled out a jar from the corner under the table. There was a butterfly in the bedroom that wasn't dead. The creature in the jar was even bluer than the eyes staring at it. Lila crouched on the floor, opened the jar and, using a tiny pair of forceps, held it by its insect-y body. "Mind?" She wanted me to hand her the tiny brown jar on the table between our beds. I just continued plucking my strings.

She sighed as if nothing more could be expected of a dimwit like me and dropped the butterfly into a third jar she had nearby, plaster in the bottom. She spread her hand over the top and walked over on her knees and got the brown jar herself. She dispensed several drops from it onto the blue wings. It smelled like tenth grade biology, like dead sea anemones and frogs pinned open, the alimentary canal, heart and lungs removed.

Lila waited. Then unscrewed the jar and tipped the dead butterfly into her hand. The room seemed to have a blue tinge to it now, as if someone had colored the fixture in the ceiling. I closed my eyes. I didn't move off the bed they were loaning me. Popped my strings and kept time with my bare foot, a small foot, the secret part of my father. All anyone ever noticed were my dark Mexican eyes.

"It's a Blue Morpho," Lila said. "The chrysalis came by mail over a week ago. I've been feeding it rotten fruit to keep it alive. This one's a male. The females are nothing special. If you ever see a picture of a Morpho on a flower with his wings open, they've just taken him out of the refrigerator. Unless they're cold, they close their wings at rest."

I continued popping my heavy gauge strings. I was just fooling around, hardly listening to her. "Where's your Cabbage White?"

In spring my mom's little planter box of mint and basil would be covered with the small white butterflies.

Lila turned away. She was already bored with me. "Last spring I was supposed to audition for the ballet company in Portland," she said, arranging the butterfly on a block of wood on top of her glass case. "I'm that good. Unfortunately, they put me in the hospital. A temporary setback. I'm a dancer, is what I'm saying. I only surround myself with beauty. The Cabbage White is scrappy, I'll give you that. It arrived in North America, most likely in a shipment of grain from Europe in the later 1800's, and spread, positively like *wild fire*, from coast to coast. People call it a moth because then it's easier to kill. It's a pest, Gwen. The butterfly can survive anywhere, but that doesn't make it pretty. Don't make me say this again."

Seven

Two weeks of school were in the can. Too many remained to think about. I knew when I left Friday I'd done about perfect on my geometry test, and Monday our teacher handed them back and we were supposed to pass them to the guy in front of us to grade. If he was your buddy, he put his arm down on the desk and erased your definitions and wrote in the correct answers Miss So-and-So was busy writing on the blackboard. This was going on with all the football players in the back of the room. Some of them were here for the second year in a row. Everybody had to pass geometry to graduate.

My teacher patted her hair, gathered in a bun high on the back of her head, and asked for the definition of a scalene triangle.

Up went my hand. "It has no congruent sides."

"And an isosceles triangle?" She chewed on her melon-colored lip and scanned our faces.

"It has at least two sides that are equal," I blabbed.

"Gwen, give the others a chance."

Behind me, Dennis Bly snickered with the guy across the aisle, both of them runners. "What a suck-up," he whispered loudly.

I spun around and looked the guy square in his gold eyeballs. "How are all your eggs doing these days?"

He wore black leather gloves day in, day out, they were his trademark. He put one of them over his mouth now and whispered, "Hey, write that in," nodding at the correct answer for the definition of a polygon our teacher in her breezy linen suit was writing on the board.

My pencil got busy writing minus fives in the margin of Dennis's test. Then I tore off a corner (he hadn't used much paper) and wrote "You need any help out there at the salmon hatchery? I know someone who needs a job," and I passed the note over my shoulder.

I caught my teacher's eye and smiled, alert and ready to provide the next answer, but she looked to someone else. We were all juniors and seniors, mostly boys, kids who had fallen behind in math somewhere along the line. I didn't need anybody to cheat for me on a test this easy. The boy in front was writing plus fives everywhere across my paper.

I felt Dennis's finger in my back. "Will you give me a break, Pérez? I'm going to flunk."

I spun around and peeled my silvery blonde hair out of my face. "Who do I talk to at the hatchery?"

"Who says there's work?"

"Gwen? Dennis?" The lady at the blackboard frowned

and felt to see if the collar of her linen jacket was lifted. (It was). "How did you two get the impression this is social hour?"

"Ma'am," Dennis said huffily. "If I was socializing with Gwen Pérez, I apologize. She's not my type."

Behind us the guys who carried the football around the field snickered into their bellies. I dropped my face. I felt the woman gazing at me, at the top of my head, but I kept my eyes down until I heard her chalk digging into the board again.

There were three more questions to go. I picked up my pencil and wrote "zero" on top of Dennis's test.

"Come on," he whispered.

I wrote FUCK YOU in my notebook and held it up high so he and everyone behind me could see.

"OK, someone else make a stab at it. What makes this triangle obtuse?" The lady sidled down the wall, her chunky necklace swinging as she bent and jabbed her finger at one of the seniors in the back of the room, a linebacker or something, one of those low-profile positions. "You. Define an obtuse angle."

An angle over ninety degrees, I wanted to shout, but Dennis was mumbling a name under his breath. Scott something.

"It's pretty hard work, Pérez."

I changed several minus signs to pluses. Did I get a thanks out of the guy? All was silence behind me.

Eight

When Dennis found me at lunch he repeated himself. "It's pretty wet work out there, Pérez. Don't you work for that feminist already? Are you into cleaning and scrubbing raceways? Someone like you probably thinks of that as housework."

The word *Stihl* was sewn across the front of his ball cap. Like most of the boys at school he liked to advertise the people who made chain saws.

"That was an easy test, Dennis. Are you dumb or lazy?" I leaned back and swallowed milk.

"I'll repeat myself, Pérez, because I guess you didn't hear. It's pretty hard work out at the hatchery. It's not really the place for a girl."

"*Mierda.*" I set my carton down carefully. I didn't normally lapse into my father's language. I wasn't good at it. This moment seemed to call for it.

"I already have a job, Dennis. I practically run Miz Hundy's show barn. I want the job for Lila Abernathy."

Trays slammed onto tables around us. Laughter bounced off the tiled walls. Across the room, Lila in her yellow scarf was watching us. She took geometry last year, passed it I don't know how, being as she got sick just as spring arrived, and vanished to the hospital across the river. Smart, I guess.

"Lila needs to get out in the fresh air, Dennis, but if you don't hire girls, what can we do."

"Since when are you two buddies?"

"She broods over her collection of dead insects every afternoon, Dennis. She arranges them like furniture. It's morbid."

Some big guys moved in to buy Cokes and then leaned against the machine. I could no longer see Lila.

Dennis shifted uncomfortably. "How's she doing?"

"No." I shook my head. "You clear up your guilty conscience on your own. Go ask her if you're curious. Now—" I lifted my glasses and socked the boy in the chops with my black Mexican gaze. "You either need someone or you don't. And I heard you lost your other part-timer. So that means you do. Need someone."

The guy had a narrow face, high cheekbones, as if he had an Indian ancestor along in there somewhere. His neck and hands were tanned from other summers, certainly not the cold, wet one we'd just had. He had gold eyes like the ones in my lost cat, and a bad haircut, but he was good-looking, all right. I could see why Lila would ask him to a dance. There was something restless about the guy, and maybe a little sweet at his center, like one of those sour candies that turn sugary and wonderful if you suck on them long enough. A year ago Lila had clung to the edge of popularity. She was capable of throwing herself against a sheer, vertical surface like this guy and holding on for dear life. She never got to the sweet part of him, though, before she got sick and left town. I wondered, even as I sat there, if Connie Beller had reached Dennis's center. If she'd tried.

"We're about to spawn early Coho and you're right," he nodded, "we're short-handed. Can Lila swing a baseball bat?"

I watched my pasta ice over. "She's pretty good at standing on the ends of her toes. Does that count?"

"Next time, don't be such a hardass with my test." Dennis sauntered back to the center table and dropped in beside that foreign country, Connie Beller, his arm settling over her shoulders, proudly, I thought. The bell rang and the whole group of them jumped up and left their trays, as if their mothers were coming to pick up after them.

I dropped my tray on the cart and pushed through the double doors, into the hall.

"There's a five. Naw, give her a six." The guys from the back of math class were lined shoulder to shoulder outside the cafeteria. They referred to a senior from the trailers who walked by with her books up at her chest. I watched her push through them, the big guys jostling and blocking her. They always treated loggers' daughters this way. I'd live up the highway myself if old Mrs. Tooney hadn't died when I was a kid. My mom and me packed our stuff into our truck and drove into town and spent ten pretty good years together in the old lady's apartment, the beauty shop one floor below us.

I turned and slipped back into the cafeteria. The women closing down the line gave me looks. You weren't supposed to step behind the stainless steel servers, but oh, well. Out the side door I went into gray September.

Nine

Walking home that afternoon I cut behind the school, around behind the pool, across our tennis courts with cracks and potholes, broken ankles in the making, and through several hundred yards of thickly growing Doug fir, which took me out of my way, almost to the hospital, but this way I didn't have to pass Edgar Fuentes's gas station. That morning he'd been wearing his hat, green on his black hair. I'd told him I was ashamed of it. Did he listen?

I came out at Fifth and Main. Son of a gun if I didn't hear someone calling me. Lila Abernathy clattered up the sidewalk as fast as she could in her silly pumps. The girl was smoking. It must have been a hard week for her.

I was flattered she'd chosen my brand (my mom's actually), only she'd gotten Pall Mall menthols, not my favorite.

"What were you saying to Dennis Bly at lunch?" she demanded, breathing hard. "I saw you two talking."

"Got an extra cig?"

She passed me one and I lit up. I turned my head to blow smoke at the passing trucks. "What'd you ever see in a fucker like Dennis Bly?"

"He's good enough for the most popular girl in school." She turned away, her excitement draining out of her.

"On your one and only date with him he was a perfect gentleman, wasn't he? Or that's what you tell yourself to explain why he didn't touch you."

Her pretty mouth tightened.

"Of all the nerve," I continued. "In class today he said I'm not his type."

"You're very rude."

"Connie Beller lives in the biggest house in town, Lila, just in case you've forgotten. Do you think they're allowed to do it in her bedroom?"

"Fuck off, Gwen."

The air between us prickled with tension. I stepped carefully away from her, the hair up on my arms, and took off down the sidewalk, moving gracelessly, but covering ground.

Mrs. Parker made good money cleaning houses. She worked on a team with two other ladies. They moved in like a whirlwind and finished a three-story home on the bluff in two hours. It had to burn calories. Most afternoons she was home around this time, soaking in the tub. She'd come out in her black robe with a dragon embroidered across her heavy shoulders and matching black slippers, with her hair in a towel, to start dinner. Not today, though. She was late and there was nobody to cluck their tongue when I gulped in a deep breath, said now or never, and swung up behind the wheel of the blue Chevy. My hands on the steering wheel wiped that little bit of my mom from the surface of my life. I rubbed her prints off on my jeans and drove to the end of the street. The white guardrail had a dent in it from someone's fender. Long yellow grass heavy with seeds hung over it. Across the field was the river that passed our town day in, day out.

Coming up the other side of the street all the houses had big, staring windows and porches easing their way toward earth. Most people were still at the mill or they'd left for the evening shift to wait tables, and the street was easy to drive down. I took a left at the stop sign, just as Lila turned in, her heels and bad mood slowing her.

I hit fifty leaving town, didn't touch the box of my mom's Pall Malls sliding around on the dash. Her Wrigley's on the seat. (L.D. didn't like my mother smoking.) In back was the spare. Several deep breaths brought me nothing. She was never big on perfume. I decided it would be all right to roll down the window.

The west end of town was marked by a tiny restaurant where Lila's mom used to work, wheedling tips out of loggers who lived farther up the highway. ThenWeyerhaeuser land on both sides of the road for several miles, then the white fences of Flying Horse Shoe Stables arrived. This part of my life hadn't changed, anyway.

I turned up my boss's rutted road toward her big show barn, where a dozen thoroughbreds were stalled and pampered. I parked on the south side of the barn under a huge old hemlock. When I slid the heavy outer door open nickers and little snorts of greeting filled the breezeway. All the way down the line of stalls, ears were pricked and heads were raised up behind the grills in the Dutch doors. I hollered one general hello, but saved personal greetings for later.

I cut through the feed room and crossed the packed dirt to the arena. Laid my arms on her white board fence. The woman herself stood in the middle of the packed sawdust, waving a cigarette at a sixth- or seventh-grade girl on Chastity, a pretty pinto mare and one of our best lesson horses. She was yelling at the girl to *feel* her diagonals and quit looking down. "Look who's here," she shot at me. "If I wasn't knee-deep in work, Gwen, I'd invite you into my camper for a nip of whiskey. Welcome back."

The girl's mother frowned, standing off to the left, trying to keep her shoes clean.

I wrapped my hands around the fence and waited while Miz Hundy told her student to sit up straighter and watch her horse's shoulder. She tugged off her helmet. She'd colored her hair since my mom's funeral. It had those brassy tones again and she'd skimped on conditioner.

"Christ, look at him, Gwen. Look what I've got to deal with."

I turned to follow her pointing finger. A horse was corralled between her camper and the north side of the barn. Robust and leggy with a rich brown coat and girlish blond mane and tail, the animal slammed himself into the steel bars of the enclosure. His body was built large and strong, but he'd been cut from especially fine cloth, you could see the quality of his bloodlines in his nostrils and ears, the perfect curve of his long back, the muscle pack in his hindquarters. I couldn't stop staring at him, even as he continued to ram himself into steel with no apparent idea of quitting. Self-abuse in any form fascinates me.

"Gallant was delivered this morning," Miz Hundy murmured. "Right off the track. I got him from Yakima—cheap—he's got a mental block against winning. Was I crazy to buy him?"

"What are you going to do with him?" I asked.

"Turn him into a gorgeous big jumper. Things were getting boring around here, weren't they?" She chuckled. "The vet's coming with a tranquilizer. You can't get near him. Once he calms down, though, I'll expect you to give him the same TLC you give the others, Gwen. You are back for good? I can depend on you?"

Miz Hundy dropped her cigarette butt under her boot heel, making more work for me. The corral rails twanged, groaned and held. The horse opened his throat and shrieked. Whinnies echoed up and down the length of the barn.

"He's going to stir them all up," my boss murmured.

"Why couldn't you have spent your money on a Hanoverian mare schooled in dressage with third-level movements under her belt, Miz Hundy?"

"I don't remember you being such a wet blanket, Gwen. Don't go near him. Just call the vet, tell him I don't pay him to pussyfoot around. I need his tail out here."

The lady started toward her student and the young mare. "Get her into a working trot, honey, start posting. I want you to quit looking down."

My footsteps echoed down the length of the horse barn. The breezeway was concrete and the stalls, dirt. Refreshing four inches of sawdust for each horse once a week was my never-ending job, not to mention the daily tasks of picking up manure, grooming, and feeding.

One wall of the tack room was covered with equipment that always gave me a thrill to look at. Neatly-coiled lead ropes, longe lines, rope halters. Bridles with silver-studded head stalls and complicated curb bits for the sensitive mouths of show horses. A lot of girls preferred snaffles for the elegant way they looked and because, by wearing one in the ring, you could sometimes fool a judge into thinking your horse was more obedient than it was. The egg-butt, D-ring, and full-cheek snaffles were popular. Miz Hundy's motto was, use the simplest bit to achieve your goal—above all, have kind hands.

In the small tool room I got my blue wheelbarrow, rake and shovel. The fat old mare, Red, was swishing her thick sorrel tail when I pulled up outside her stall. She thought she was getting turned out.

I hadn't been out here since my mother died. A lot of pretty complicated feelings hit me hard. Memories were dragged up from the place I had stamped them down. Her big and capable hands closing her account book on her shop counter, her eyes watering when she plucked her eyebrows, how she'd stand in the middle of the kitchen and peer into a pot lid. "Honey? Am I getting old?"

I tied Red out to the hitching post. She wasn't happy with that arrangement, she wanted to get out in the pasture and frolic. She was old but still beautiful and in her heart she was a filly. I told her, no can do. The pastures near the highway had been reseeded and she couldn't set foot in either one till spring. One of these days Miz Hundy would clear the rest of her land. One of these days.

I had moved on to Sir, a sturdy dappled gray with excellent form over the jumps, and one of the barn's few geldings, when Connie Beller threw her arm over the half door. "*Como estas?*"

She knew my father was Mexican. She liked to show off

her Spanish. She didn't know how to say "Cute necklace," though. She said that in English.

"You say that every time I wear it." I emptied my shovel-load of manure into the wheelbarrow. "I'm going to get the idea you think I wear it too often, Connie."

The jewelry she was complimenting was a thick piece of silver that lay nicely, I thought, on my collarbone. My present from my mom for turning sixteen last May.

"Agnes looks good," she replied, naming her own birthday present, the year before last.

"Just good? Not excellent?"

"I saw that new horse in the corral."

I eyeballed Connie. She was the great-or-whatever granddaughter of the amateur butterfly collector who founded our town. He was big into timber too, of course, but it was his butterfly collection they held at the library. In elementary school we took a field trip to stare at it. That must have been how Lila got the idea. This ancestor gave Connie a certain advantage. She had talent for organizing and bossing girls. She'd been top dog since elementary school. She was probably the reason Lila had lost her friends. I couldn't dismiss her completely, though, because she jumped her horse with care and precision and was utterly fearless in the show ring.

"Agnes is not going to be happy," Connie continued. "She likes being the most beautiful horse in the barn."

"No, Isabella gets that honor," I said, naming the dark mahogany bay a few stalls down.

"You're just partial to old Red and her daughters." Connie smiled.

"One thing we *can* say about your horse, Connie, she's most likely to get injured."

"A bowed tendon could happen to anyone."

"Gallant's fresh off the track and not happy about it," I said. "Don't go near him."

"What's Miz Hundy going to do with him?"

I clanked my shovel against the wheelbarrow. "Maybe make you ride him."

"I have a horse."

"Yeah. How long since you've ridden her?"

Lots of bowed horses recover and lead athletic lives, Gwen." Connie stepped back and pulled off her helmet, shaking out her thick blonde hair. Whereas I had something of Miz Hundy's old weathered barn in my shade of blonde, streaks of ash, you could say, Connie's hair was absolutely golden, like rich butter.

"I guess you heard my brother's home from Philadelphia?"

"Got kicked out, I heard." I struck a match and ran the thumb of my hand with the cigarette up and down a two by four in the unfinished wall.

"You're surrounded by guys I wouldn't shake a stick at, Connie. Your boyfriend. Your spoiled brat brother. Did he bring home his expensive violin?"

"Ooh. Wait till my mother hears you said that."

I had no time to think about Lynn Beller, or those couple of days I'd lived with Connie's family in their mansion on the bluff east of high school. That was the bad summer when I turned fourteen and Edgar Fuentes came back to town, smelling of suntan lotion. That was the summer my mom and I started to argue as if someone was paying us by the hour. My boss handed me her snorting mare's reins. "Cool her out," she ordered, as if I didn't know what to do with a blowing, hot horse. The middle-school girl had already circled the barn. I heard a car door slam, wheels on gravel.

Miz Hundy linked arms with Connie. She told her gently but firmly, her horse wasn't available, how about putting Sir over some jumps instead? "Come on, not the long face," Miz Hundy said cheerfully. "Sir's a love in the ring. I'll help you tack him up. Gwen's busy."

I smoked in the stall with the sweating mare and listened to them. People in this town were screwing up left and right. Arthur Beller was back home? The guy was an ass, but talented. The high point of living with the Bellers those couple of days was hearing Connie's brother imitate his violin god, Jascha Heifetz. Arthur was supposed to be starting his second year at his hotshot conservatory back east. So. My life wasn't the only one that had jumped the track.

To block out the wheedling tone in my boss's voice and to rid myself of the heaviness that, since my mom died, always seemed to settle on me about dusk, I headed for the new horse.

The barn lights had come on. The coat on the animal's back and hindquarters looked fine, but his chest was matted with blood and the skin had broken in several places. The light buzzing on the pole made this perfectly clear, but I couldn't tell if the damage was partly from a human hand or entirely the beating the horse had inflicted on himself.

His neck arched with rage.

"I'm responsible for many things," I told him, "but not your confinement. You'd be in a European sandwich right now if you weren't so good-looking. They like horse meat across the Atlantic. Couldn't pull your act together to win a single race, eh?"

I dropped my Pall Mall under my boot heel and reached

over the top bar and swiftly clipped the rope I was holding onto the ring of the horse's halter. I lifted the latch and
stepped sideways. The thoroughbred slammed out as if the
bell had rung. I had two strong arms from all the shoveling of manure and hauling of hay I'd done in the last two
years. The horse dragged me twenty feet. He stopped short
near Miz Hundy's neat white fence that bounded her north
pasture. He tossed his finely-shaped head, as if he was surprised to find me still attached. He pranced sideways, trying to shake me off.

I informed the tempestuous creature that my mom often
felt the same way about me. Ever since that bad summer, she
wanted to put a ten foot pole between us. Unfortunately, we
lived in a tiny, tiny apartment above her beauty shop in the
center of town. "That's why she sent me to the Bellers," I told
him. "Only I came right back home."

The horse stopped. Was he listening to me? His ears
were up. He was focused on the dense trees across the
fence. Maybe he'd never seen Doug fir growing this thick
before. Maybe the smell intoxicated him. The reins were
coiled around my arm (stupidly). I started walking toward
the barn.

I vaguely heard Miz Hundy yelling at me but I didn't pay
much attention. As much as I'd been around horses, this
one was doing something I'd only seen in movies. He
pawed the air above my head. He balanced whole seconds
on rear hoofs that weren't made for his kind of weight. His
hoofs were delicate and small for his size and I watched
them approach my face, upturned and staring as if I'd
slipped away from time. Then I was on the ground and
pain tore out in all directions from my shoulder.

"Fuck," I informed the dark sky that seemed to have

drawn closer. I didn't move. Everything be damned. I felt the vibrations in the earth as the horse galloped off. If he was running toward the highway, that was his problem.

All I could see of Miz Hundy's face was her wide open mouth. The woman was roaring at me.

"I'm fine," I heard myself say.

"You jackass. Didn't I tell you to leave the horse alone?"

In the arena lights I could see the way her jowls hung loose as a dog's. I thought she was going to hit me. Kick me. I didn't move to defend myself.

This lady had booked my mother and grandmother in her tavern years ago, a duo, giving the Singing Trees their first break. Long, long ago, before my grandmother had a heart attack and my mother got married to a drifter to heal her own damaged heart.

"My last request before I die is a cig." I was propped up now on a bale of hay in the feed room. My sweatshirt was torn open. My shoulder looked strangely chewed, ached fiercely.

"I think it's broken," I said. "How come it's not bleeding?"

Pretty Connie frowned in the doorway. "Is someone going to catch that horse? He's over by the far fence."

"Do you see anyone else with free hands?" Miz Hundy snapped. "Never mind. I'll do it. You'd better not get near him. Gwen, I'll get whiskey." She pulled her hand away and I timbered into the stud wall. Her riding boots clattered on the steps of her camper that doubled as a waiting room for mothers.

All the way into the emergency room Miz Hundy filled my ear. I couldn't follow directions if she paid me. Couldn't I see the horse was hopped up and needed a tranquilizer? Where was her damn vet? How would I feel if I'd been hauled on an open stock truck all the way from eastern Washington? She ought to fire me, if I couldn't follow directions. Miz Hundy's time was valuable. On and on. She'd poured Jim Beam in a glass for me. The whiskey peeled my throat. I hoped I had my voice the next time I needed it. That and my hair were the only things I had from my mom.

I had dislocated my shoulder. The doctor explained this as he worked a mint around inside his cheek. I felt like telling him I didn't do it, Miz Hundy's hedge against boredom did. He said he'd pop my shoulder back in place as soon as the muscles relaxed. "We have to get these shoulder muscles very, very relaxed," he explained, "so I can yank on you a bit." He laced his hands together and cracked his knuckles.

A piece of skin hung through the cotton of my sweatshirt. My blood vessels had been shattered. My shirt was damp with blood now, and he didn't seem in the least concerned. I thought of what our cat Lou used to leave in piles under the coffee table when my mother and I went at it late at night these last couple of years. She'd run for toilet paper. "Poor cat has a sensitive stomach like me, quit yelling." I'd reply, I wasn't yelling. "Quit saying you weren't yelling," and I'd be left in the kitchen with my cold coffee and old Mrs. Tooney's strange green walls.

In her riding jacket and jodhpurs Miz Hundy looked her usual intimidating self, fidgeting by the curtain. "You know the world we live in, Doctor," she barked. "The premium our culture places on feminine beauty. Will the girl have a scar?"

Her question seemed to pause the man in his tracks. He pulled mints from his blue hospital pants. Pressing his thumbnail, he popped one off the roll.

"We can't suture these kinds of injuries, I'm afraid. Oh, yes, Ma'am. She will have a scar."

Ten

We idled at the curb below Mrs. Parker's yellow house. Ought she come up and explain the situation? My arm in a sling, Miz Hundy meant.

She lifted her hand off the steering wheel and brushed hair out of her plain, strong-boned face.

"She has more different crosses she wears," I said under my breath. "She gave me one. I'll never wear it." The knot the doctor had tied at my neck felt too tight.

Miz Hundy was quiet so long I started to wonder if I'd offended her. "We're going to have to clear out your apartment soon, Gwen. I've got a few potential renters. As far as the crucifix, she gives me one every Christmas."

I sucked in a breath. "What about the shop?"

"Nobody I'm crazy about."

"You're not going to rent to Lonna Caruthers?"

"You know perfectly well I'm not."

I almost smiled. "That would make my mom happy."

"I don't make my decisions with your mother in mind."

"OK, but even so, I'm going to go up there to the cemetery and tell her you're not renting to Lonna, her main competitor in this town."

The woman shook her head. "I hate to see you do that."

"Pay my respects to her?"

"How long have you been working for me now, Gwen? Two years and more? I'm getting to know you. Every decision you make, I see you weighing it to make sure it's nothing your mother would do. You live too cautiously. I don't believe you know how to have fun. There's more to life than caring for my horses. Don't be offended by me saying this. You've become terribly conservative."

"First, I don't think you really know me, Miz Hundy. Second, my mother is hardly buried, I don't think it's time for singing and dancing."

"I've hurt your feelings. That wasn't my intention. It's just, are you going to be a long time mourning her, do you think? I don't mean to sound cold. If you could see what the rest of us see. That's all."

"I can't believe you're saying this to me." I put my shoulder, the uninjured one, to the car's heavy door.

"Gwen—"

I slammed the door shut with my boot. I felt her watching me all the way up her sister's front steps. To hell with her.

"She sends you back to me like this? Is this supposed to be funny? What happened to your arm?" Mrs. Parker took her white shirt off the ironing board, shook it, and slipped it on a hanger.

"I got Lila a job." I hadn't moved off the rug, just inside the front door.

Nona Parker bent over and inspected the pleats in her brown tweed skirt. "You what?"

"At the salmon hatchery. Well, I'm on the road to getting her an interview, anyway. She can't spend all her free time in her room. Is that where she is now?"

"Your dinner's in the oven, and I'm waiting for an explanation about that arm."

I swept past her. "It looks worse than it is."

A piece of foil covered my plate on the top rack of the oven. Even one-handed, it took only a few minutes to leave a pile of chicken bones.

I looked up to see Mrs. Parker watching me from the doorway. She pushed her roll of hair out of her sweaty face. "Does this mean you and Lila are getting along?"

"Why is it so important we get along?"

"A divided house falls, Gwen."

"Mrs. Parker!"

I got up and banged my plate into the garbage. My week for dishes. I'd have to do them one-handed. They'd already eaten. Their plates were stacked neatly in the left side of the sink. I turned on the water, wishing she had a radio on her counter. That's one thing I'd save from our stuff on Ninth Street.

"Mrs. Parker?"

"Yes?" she called from the living room.

I went in there. Wiped my hand on my jeans. "Did you know Arthur Beller's home?"

"You know I clean their house. How could I not know?"

"If anyone had a chance to make it, it was him."

"His poor sister, on the phone, from what I understand,

just about morning, noon and night, trying to get them to take him back."

"Helpful of Connie."

"Looking out for her brother when all her mother does is shop." Mrs. Parker shook her head.

"Mrs. Beller was a good customer, though, to my mom." The woman didn't answer.

"What did Arthur do?" I asked.

"I don't traffic in gossip, Gwen."

"Then you don't pay attention to what people around town are saying about my mother? That she was driving too fast around that corner?"

Mrs. Parker pulled her brown skirt off the ironing board and shook it out and pinned it on her hanger. "Your mother," she sighed. "Always in a hurry. Everything about her saddens me."

"God, warn me before you say something like that next time." I headed back into the kitchen, blinking hard.

"You have to face this, Gwen," Mrs. Parker called. "She lived recklessly."

"L.D. liked her," I shouted back, running the tap.

"Look what it's done to him. Look what it's done to the man! Leaving his week's wages in my sister's tavern!"

I shut off the tap and rubbed chicken grease off the woman's china. "She says I live too cautiously. Your sister. She doesn't really know me."

"Oh, for heaven's sake," Mrs. Parker bellowed. "I'm going to have a talk with her."

I changed the subject. "She has a new horse," I called. "I got too close. That's what happened to me."

"She's too old for men, I suppose."

Crossing the kitchen, I stopped in the doorway. She was

still at her ironing board, her back to me. "What's that supposed to mean?" I said.

"I'm human, Gwen. I get tired. I say things."

Her black robe was tightly belted. The dragon across her
broad back was embroidered in deep green and gold. Her
feet were bare. Her matching slippers were over by the
door.

"Injured as you are, leave the rest of the dishes," the
woman said without turning around. "I'll finish them."

Eleven

I had the dream again that night. I was in the river with my mom. We were belted into the little Corvette, the current spun us around. The river was pitch-black, but a light came from the dash. The radio was playing that California dreaming song. I leaned forward and turned the dial. The song was on every station. I knew it was a dream because I could breathe. We had enough air in our lungs to argue.

"You stink like the swimming pool," my mother said.

"We're in the river, not the pool, Mom. Why are we in the river? You didn't land in the river."

"I said you stink like the pool and you do. A woman my age can't adore a man the way you do, honey, not with a straight face."

"I never get in the water. I just sit on the bleachers. The

chlorine's bad for my hair. How many times have you told me that?"

"I have a conditioner you should give him. You're in love with him, I suppose."

"I'm knitting him a hat. I've got it in four pieces."

My mom unsnapped her belt and floated out of the passenger seat toward the ceiling. I heard a clink and realized she held a drink in her long and fluid-looking hand.

"If you give him anything, *any*thing, Gwen, he'll never leave town." Her long blonde hair floated toward me and my own hair moved out to meet hers. I couldn't tell where her hair stopped and mine started. Bubbles came out of our mouths.

"I don't want him to leave, Mom."

"You will."

"Did you get tired of Gustavo? Is that why he left?"

"I would have."

"You always have a smart answer, Mother. I'm going now." I grabbed the window crank. All I got was my head in the river before she grabbed me and tugged me back into the car. "Where do you think you're going? That's right. I'm your mother. I'm not finished."

I opened my mouth. Water felt silky in my throat. I tried to remember the sensation because I knew I was dreaming. Then I was staring into the cold white light of the moon. The sky had cleared and white light poured down on me. I thought of the hospital, lifted my shoulder and winced. I turned to see Lila's bald head on her pillow. Then clouds moved in, the room went dark.

Someone was singing outside. A woman's voice that rose and fell in a language beyond this town. Hair lifted on my arms. I longed to return to my dream. I'd tell my mother I'd be good. I'd break up with Edgar Fuentes. She was right. He was old enough to be my father. I'd never spend another night behind the gas station in his cramped, smelly van. I'd give her peace so she could collect her thoughts and remember the self she'd lost years and years ago, before she'd met my father, before I was born.

The woman continued singing dark and lonely things. Even from across the street her tone was pure and her high notes were more impressive than mine would ever be. Sleep had vanished. I might as well get a look at this Dr. Kazlowski.

I wore a tank top and sweats for pajamas. My usual. I leaned down for my work boots, thrown into the space between our beds. Clawed as gently as I could at the stretchy fabric holding my arm in a sling. My arm swung free and the pain didn't get any worse, which is what I'd figured. Doctors always went the extra mile in the caution department.

Lila took ages waking up. Finally, I had to flip on the light. "What's so special about your dreams?" I murmured, watching her struggle up off her pillow, rubbing her eyes.

She yawned and stared at me. Without her scarf she looked incredibly young or old, I couldn't decide which.

"I'm going to pay a visit to the doctor," I explained. "Come on." My heavy coat hung over the dressing-table chair.

"We're not allowed." She wrapped her thin arms around her knees.

Standing on my bed in my work boots, I turned again to look at her. "This is the bold attitude that will get you on stage? Lila?"

Then I was out the window, crushing a rhododendron, grabbing at it with my good arm to stop my fall. The houses on Mrs. Parker's side were built on a small hill, and the grass was slick. I waited for her on the sidewalk. "Lila!" I called softly. My shoulder ached to the bone.

Gilbert Street was quiet. Here and there a light on a pole did what it could to push back the night. Cathlamet Indians had camped right here in the front yard once. They would have stayed near the river. All dead now, of course, from malaria and other white man diseases, but I thought for an instant I could feel them around me, bending over their cooking fires, turning strips of salmon. No sign of Lila. Oh, well.

I skirted potholes. Music was coming from the front of the pink house but its windows were dark. The empty flowerboxes looked forlorn in the poor light. His yellow car crowded his tiny, weedy lawn. Lights were on around back. My coat caught a couple of times on the neighbor's hedge. I found the man himself reclining in a lawn chair underneath blazing patio lights.

"Jesus." He sprang to his feet. "You are—who, exactly?"

"Someone really ought to trim up this hedge." I tugged my coat free. "Gwen Pérez, your neighbor."

"A fan of Giuseppe Verdi, are you?" He squinted at me. "Well, my dear,"—he had recovered fast from his surprise—"*La Traviata* is one of the most beloved operas in the world, though, I must confess, it's terribly over the top. A lot of bluster about very little." He spoke playfully, grabbing the other lawn chair and tipping off water. He patted the seat. "I don't normally entertain young ladies at this hour. But you're here, sit down then."

I glanced over my shoulder. "My friend's coming."

"Oh?"

"She's probably using the front door."

The man wore track shorts and loafers and a T-shirt he'd

probably owned since he was my age. He was so tall and bony I felt that I was in the company of a moving, talking tree.

His lawn chair felt hard as concrete. I drew my knees to my chin but that only interfered with my shoulder, so I stretched out my legs and tried to relax. I was nervous. A couple of beer cans rolled off his picnic table.

He asked me what I wanted to drink. "Here." He bent over and tugged a space heater closer to me. He had a heater out here. I popped up and, using my good arm, moved the awkward chair around, bending nearer to the warm air.

The doorbell rang loud and clear into the backyard. "That's her," I said. "Lila."

"Couldn't be the Avon lady?"

"I'll lay money you have a girl with a yellow scarf on your front step."

"Oh, the very pretty girl? In remission from leukemia, I understand. Her Portland doctors have her on a somewhat daring clinical trial."

"Well, you use your eyes, anyway." I turned away and leaned back against my chair.

When the man returned Lila trailed him. I could see what had taken her so long. She had applied a full face of make-up. He waved at his lawn chair and told her to sit down. Lila continued to stand.

"What can I offer you to drink? Please say coffee, it's all I have."

"Won't that stunt our growth?" Lila said.

"Bring it on then," I replied. "Make it to grow hair on our chests."

The man vanished through his patio door.

"Makeup?" I hissed at Lila.

"Look at that." She nodded at the half case on the picnic table.

"If you can't deal with it you'd better go," I scoffed. "I can't believe Miz Hundy says I don't take risks. Look at me. I'm here. I'm acting bold. I take plenty of risks. I can't *believe* you're wearing makeup, Lila."

The man reappeared, empty-handed, before I could continue down that path. Lila sat on the edge of his lawn chair now, so he settled on his picnic bench. He popped open a Coors.

"Don't you work in the emergency room?" she inquired politely. "I think Mrs. Parker said that."

He nodded at the beer. "I've got this little problem, so they've put me on nights. Nights and more nights."

"But not tonight?" she said. Even here she couldn't keep from moving her foot around and around in one of her little ballet exercises.

"They give him some nights off, fool." The man had a mop of hair with its best days behind it. Gray, gray.

"Doctor, if you're a, you know—" I nodded at the carton of beer. "I guess it's a good thing my shoulder got dislocated during the day, when the other doctor could pop it back."

He perked up. "What's that?"

"The doctor who likes breath mints. He popped my shoulder back this afternoon."

"Christ." He swallowed beer and threw the can against his house. "I'm twice the physician Bix is. I'd better have a look at his work." He opened the patio door with his elbow. "Come in."

"Don't, Gwen," Lila hissed.

I was already on my feet.

"He's going to make you take your clothes off."

I thought it over. "Jealous?"

The lady's voice had faded on the tape player in the man's living room. His was about three times the size of the one I had at the barn. Cassettes and CDs were stacked on it. Beside it, leaning against his bare wall, was a backpack on a steel frame and a neat coil of rope that looked more hi-tech than our stuff at the barn. A couch filled the other side of the room under the window. An unmatched armchair and an old bookcase that held a couple of paperbacks completed things.

The man told me to go into the bathroom and take off my tank top. (Lila raised her eyebrows at me.) He said I could wrap a towel around my chest if I was shy, but leave my shoulder free so he could thump on me a bit. I was in there maybe three seconds when Lila joined me.

"Is the word privacy unknown to you?" I was sitting on the toilet. Maybe I was a little nervous.

"I can't believe he lives on this street," she whispered. "Do you think it's because he's an alcoholic?"

She stood at the doctor's tiny mirror, fussing with her eyeliner. Several of the tiny bulbs in the row above her head had burned out, and she looked more beautiful than ever in the dim light, all angles and bright eyes.

"Lila, I believe there's Indians camped in Mrs. Parker's front yard. Dead ones, but still."

"I mean, you'd think he'd be up on the bluff with the Bellers and them," she continued.

"I could smell their fires tonight. Just for a second, like something opened between our worlds."

"Will you for once listen to me, Gwen?"

"He probably can't hold a job long enough to save the money that address requires, Lila."

"I'm waiting, ladies," came the doctor's voice and a lot of throat clearing, other side of the door.

He didn't take long to poke and prod my shoulder. He seemed satisfied I was OK. He wanted to know why my arm wasn't in a sling.

"I took it off."

He knocked his wire frames up his nose with the back of his hand. "I would venture to say that wasn't swift of you, young lady, but to a girl your age who thinks she's invincible, that will go in one ear and fall out the other."

He went to his hall closet and rummaged around, pulled out a flashlight and a box of cleaning stuff. (I saw Ajax and sponges and thought of Mrs. Parker, asleep across the street.) He said over his shoulder that he had a triangular bandage in there somewhere.

"I'm fine," I said.

He slammed the closet door. "Well, that's the thing with a dislocation. As long as it's popped back correctly you really will be fine. At least as far as your shoulder goes. That's probably not the half of it with you, though." He gave me a long look (whatever turned him on) and vanished into his kitchen. He came back with mugs of coffee.

Lila and I were side by side on his couch, but he stayed up on his loafers. He leaned against the kitchen doorway, humming under his breath the tune that had faded off his boom box.

I groaned. "This stuff tastes like gas station coffee."

Lila peered at the doctor over the rim of her mug. "The one where Edgar Fuentes works, she means. Gwen hangs around there, Dr. Kazlowski. Used to anyway."

I stared at the girl, sitting as usual on the edge of her

cushion, as though the idea of fully relaxing into a piece of furniture hadn't been invented.

"You've been gone all summer. Like you know anything."

"I know what I hear. I have eyes too. I see how he looks at you every time we walk by. I see how you put on airs and ignore him."

The doctor carried a chair in from his kitchen and rooted it into the gold shag of his living room. He sat down and regarded us. He seemed to be waiting.

"Do you have a car besides that one out front which I hear doesn't run?" I inquired. "If you do then you know the gas station nearer into town? Corner of Fifteenth? That's Edgar in Full-Serve. Short, Mexican? Long hair on his head and hair on his chin? He drove out here from Texas with my father years ago."

"Texas," the doctor murmured. "What brought them out here to this dark corner of the world?"

"Edgar's van, Dr. Kazlowski."

"I wish I could say she wasn't always this rude," Lila said mildly, setting down her mug. "I never would have moved back here if they'd told me I'd have to live with her. I was told I'd have Mrs. Parker's house to myself. I'd have a peaceful environment to concentrate on my dancing."

"Dancing, my ass," I said.

"I don't know how much longer I'm going to stay, frankly," Lila said, speaking to the doctor and ignoring me.

"Lila used to be popular," I explained. The man sat with his elbows gouging his bare knees. His legs were fuzzy with reddish hair. (That didn't match the hair on his head.) Something stirred in me, just looking into his big, interesting face, but I had a handle on it, I wasn't about to let it flame up into anything, wasn't about to apply a faceful of makeup or anything.

"Now she's on the bottom rung of the ladder and she won't make an effort to climb," I added. "This has surprised me, actually, Dr. Kazlowski. I thought she'd climb."

"Like you climb. Why should I climb?"

"I have never in my life given two farts whether Connie Beller liked me, Lila. You, on the other hand, put a lot of weight on her opinion of you."

"That's because you prefer horses to people."

"I fail to see a problem with that."

The doctor cleared his throat. "And boys? I should think you'd both be extremely popular with them."

"Gwen's popular with older men," Lila said flatly. Her pump hung off her foot, her foot itself moving in a tiny circle. "Don't make me spell it out. Edgar Fuentes?" she added impatiently. "The man at the gas station? Doctor?"

The doctor pushed himself up and creaked into the kitchen. He came back with the half pot of coffee and refilled our mugs. Mine, rather, since Lila had hardly touched hers.

"Lila's not exactly trustworthy," I said brightly. "Don't pay any attention to her. Everything she says about me comes from a place of jealousy. What do you think about someone wearing a cross who doesn't believe in what it stands for?"

"Is that the best you can do?" Lila snorted. "I'm so wounded."

"Girls. For heaven's sake. You remind me of my marriages."

"You're married?" Lila looked thunderstruck. The top of her blouse was open. She grabbed her tiny cross and twirled it.

"Four times," the man said gravely.

"Mrs. Parker didn't tell us that!" She paused. "Did they turn you into a drinker?"

I found the question interesting, and I watched the man closely.

"Young ladies," he said, "I'll give you coffee, I'll referee your squabbles, if I had groceries in the house I'd feed you. But give and take isn't in the equation. I won't allow you two to become emotionally involved in my life, and I have no plans to get involved in yours. Been there, done that, I believe you young people say? My daughter is the only teenager I have to worry about now. I've got a long vacation on my mind. Small town ER work for six more months and I'm hitting the road." He nodded at the climbing gear in the corner, yawned and stretched.

"So," he continued, "what are your plans for the rest of the evening? Is the good woman across the street going to wake up and find her charges missing? I ask from simple intellectual curiosity."

"Are you kicking us out?" I elbowed loneliness away.

I heard the fridge door open and close in the man's kitchen. He leaned in his doorway and sipped his Coors, watching us like we were TV. When there were no more gaps between his yawns, when his face was one big groaning mouth and teeth everywhere, he dropped his can into his trash and said, "All right. If you like, sleep what's left of the night where you are. If you can desist squabbling. Don't make noise in the morning. You do have school? It's my second day off in a row and therefore precious to me."

He strode down the hall and into his tiny bathroom. The door closed. We heard the water run. I bent over to unlace my boots but Lila slugged me. "Ow," I said.

"We can't do this to Mrs. Parker."

"Do what?"

"Make her feel we prefer this man's company to hers."

"Don't we?"

"She forbade us to come over here."

"Lila, you know she knows we're young and curious."

"I'm not staying."

"Fine, fine. Goddamn." I shoved my laces into my boot and hauled up and tramped down the hall. I banged as gently as I could on the bathroom door. "Doctor?"

A long groan, then: "Yes?"

"We'll see you around."

There was no reply. The water turned back on.

Twelve

If Lila had the wherewithal to build rearing cages, I figured she could hack it at the Elochoman Salmon Hatchery,
a half hour upriver, almost to the town of Cathlamet. Each
of her plywood boxes was a foot square with a screen on
top held down carefully by broken pieces of pottery. She
installed them on the washer and dryer on the back porch.
The caterpillars were a shade off chartreuse and as days
passed they began to darken. By the end of September
they had vanished into hard brown shells like slivers of
almonds, which they'd attached by wisps of silk to the
sticks Lila had provided. Fall was here.

One night when October was still fresh, she woke me
from a sound sleep. She was down the hall in the kitchen,
bumping the wall. I heard a grunt and "God damn my
turnout, anyway." I lay in my warm bed and waited to see

if she'd wake up Mrs. Parker. Finally, I threw back my covers.

I found her holding onto one of the kitchen chairs. Her left arm was out to her side and her left foot was level with the porcelain knob on the upper cabinet. She was no longer a skinny girl who'd recently wobbled, exhausted, into her first remission from leukemia. She was a work of art. I forgot my problems and just leaned in the doorway and watched her lower her leg slowly, keeping her back to me, her shoulder blades popping out of her leotard that plunged down her back to her hard little butt. As her body relaxed her flaws became evident again. Her head (wrapped in yellow as always) was too big, her feet too long, her chest hollow. Then her foot swung out and that skinny, skinny leg was suddenly perfect for the job that was required of it. Her leg spun her body cleanly and rapidly. She stopped in the middle of her last turn as if to say, it's a piece of cake, her body balanced on the ball of her foot, arms extended. I wasn't an expert but it seemed that, for Lila, a stage was just around the corner.

"What are you staring at?" She hit the floor with a thud and turned her palms up, as if examining them for calluses.

She held herself hunched over as if braced for an attack.

I went to the sink. Took a glass from the dish drainer and filled it with water. "Don't your waking hours provide enough rehearsal time, Lila?"

"A dancer can never take her *fouettés* for granted, Gwen. Do you think I woke up Mrs. Parker?" Lila glanced nervously at the hallway. "She doesn't think I'm ready."

"She's heavily invested in making you believe that."

"Whatever that means."

"You're her work of art, Lila."

"What about you?"

"Me." I snorted. "I'm her hair shirt."

Lila hesitated. "I don't go to church with her."

"Yet."

She shook her head. "I'm too busy. I'm going to start private lessons with my teacher, get back into it really intensely. My mom said she'll pay. Auditions for the company are next April. I'll be seventeen. It's now or never. I have a lot of catch-up to do, but dancing is like riding a bike. It comes back."

I put down the glass and wiped my hand across my mouth. "How are you going to take lessons and work at the hatchery? There's a job out there with your name on it."

"You drank all the pineapple juice." Lila bent into the fridge and peered behind the milk and the jar of dill pickles. "Mrs. Parker buys that for me." She straightened up. Anger poured from her blue eyes.

"You're not the only one feeling nauseous these days, Lila. The stuff's there, I drink it."

"Nauseous? Are you kidding? On my clinical trial they give me super low doses of chemo specifically so I *don't* have nausea. I have to deal with this stupid catheter, but I'll have hair by the end of the year, early January at the latest." She narrowed her eyes. "Nauseous? Are you coming down with the flu? You know my opinion of germs."

I slapped out of the kitchen and down the hall. My blankets were still warm. I turned over and faced the wall. A draft came in from somewhere, and I shivered. Mrs. Parker was cheap with heat. After a while the low moans and *umphs* started again down the hall.

Thirteen

I changed so many answers on Dennis Bly's second geometry test that he got an A. The very next Saturday morning he sat in Mrs. Parker's kitchen, sideways, so his long legs could trip everybody. I told him I'd go down and see what was keeping Lila. He had arranged an interview for her with the hatchery manager and we were going to be late.

"What the hell are you doing?" I demanded.

The girl was sitting on her bed applying eyeliner.

"You think the nylons are too much?" She glanced at me. "Shut the door."

"For the Elochoman?"

"Oh, I'm really doing it for the hatchery."

"Fine. Go toe to toe with Connie. Try to take him away from her. This'll be worth watching."

She scowled at me. "Why else have you pushed this job on me? You want to see us fight."

My bed sagged under my weight and my arms pillowed my head nicely. I was dragging and the day was only a few hours old. Should I blame Mrs. Parker's pancakes? She made them with wheat germ and stone-ground flour. They sat in my belly like river stones. Mrs. Parker had joined a bowling team. She was determined to lose weight and find a man.

A fist hit the door. In walked Dennis. "Uh—" he stopped and looked Lila up, down and sideways. "My manager hates it if you're late."

"Did you receive an invitation to enter, Dennis?" She lowered her small silver compact to her lap. She didn't lift her eyes.

"Whose butterflies?" Dennis nodded at the dressing table.

I pointed at Lila with my elbow, but she wasted this excellent conversational opener. She just sat there, waiting for the guy to leave so she could get started on her other eye.

Dennis missed this signal. He peered intently through the glass case. "Nice collection. Where's your Cabbage White?"

"Why does everybody ask me that?" Lila snapped.

"They're in the display at the library," I pointed out. "That's why. Connie's great-whatever-grandfather collected them."

(Keeping an eye on Dennis when I mentioned his girlfriend.)

Dennis pursed his lips and shoved his hands, gloves and all, into his jeans. He seemed at a loss for words.

"We'll point that out to my boss," he said finally. "That you collect insects, Lila. Scott'll like your initiative. That's his word. As in, I'm supposed to come up with ways to keep sticks and leaves from clogging up our screens. I guess I'm supposed to stop the wind from blowing? I know smolts, Fall Chinook, that sort of thing. No offense to you, but I don't collect dead things."

Lila slipped past him, me on her tail. I got my foot into the bathroom door before she could slam it.

"Lock it," she demanded. "So he doesn't come in."

"What are you doing, Lila?"

She lifted her angora sweater over her head, careful not to dislodge her scarf. She seemed to have a closet full of these sweaters. Peeling the bandage away from her collarbone down to her hard brown nipple, she whisked it into the wastebasket under the sink. A short plastic tube protruded from her. My plan to throw her against the vertical cliff currently occupying our bedroom seemed cruel suddenly.

"I need my alcohol prep pads and my heparin, a syringe and that little plastic stick you'll find on the night table. I have to flush my catheter." She pushed her face close to the mirror and smudged the liner around her one finished eye.

"You have to do this now?" I said.

"Without a doubt."

"You're acting strange, Lila."

She turned. "With a mother like yours you're not used to a little strange behavior?"

(I decided to face up to this.) "What's so strange about my mother?"

"I just wonder if she knew about you and that man at the gas station, that's all."

"If you have something to say, Lila, say it."

"You're going to look me in the eye and say there's nothing going on between you and that man? When he stops whatever it is he's doing every time you walk by?"

Dennis stood up when I entered the bedroom, leaving a depression on my bedspread. I tried not to read anything into the fact he'd chosen my bed. I wanted to delay, keep him there. I felt weirdly giddy. Maybe Lila was right. I spent too much time around horses.

"Is Lila OK?" He gave me a questioning glance.

"Physically, or in the head? I think you'd better go." I stepped aside so he could pass. I could see her blood thinner on the nightstand, but no syringe.

"I'm not going anywhere. She has an appointment for an interview and she's already late."

"I'll drive her out in a few minutes," I whispered. "I have to work at the barn today. You're just up the highway a few miles."

"If it's going to be a few minutes, I can wait."

"What if your girlfriend finds out you were in here, sitting on my bed?"

"Connie?" He barked a laugh. I waited for him to start pawing the ground. "Something about you, Pérez, really gets under my skin. I can't put my finger on it."

"For all I know you were looking in my underwear drawer."

"You're bitter, Pérez. Not an attractive quality."

"Just because my mom's dead and Lila's got a Hickman catheter in her tit, we could surprise you, Dennis. We're the dark horses in this town." I turned away.

"Come on, now," he said, and his voice gentled. "What am I supposed to tell my boss? Is she coming or not? When he gets used to the idea, he'll like having a girl. He can pay her nothing."

I stood in the hall to let him out, keeping my back to him. I felt him hesitate. "That's a professional collection she has."

"Did you hear that, Lila?" I said.

No reply from the bathroom.

After he left I put my mouth to the door. "I'll wait for you on the porch." The door winged opened. Lila grabbed the little bottle I held. "The other stuff's in the bag by my bed," she said and closed the door.

I made it to the porch in time to see Dennis pull out in his shiny new Toyota extended cab his dad bought him. That was another thing kids talked about. How a gyppo logger who worked with a couple of other guys in a town totally dominated by Weyerhaeuser, the tree-growing company, could buy his kid a rig like that. I rarely weighed in on gossip, but I had to wonder. The truck even had tow hooks in front.

Dennis didn't look up at me as he passed.

It was getting near eleven o'clock by now. A steady wind came off the river and bowed the grass over the guardrail. The wind whipped the hair off Dr. Kazlowski's shoulders where he sat in a chair behind his yellow Volkswagen. I started down the steps.

"Morning," I said, kicking the curb. "And that's all I'm saying. Just good morning."

The man pressed his thumb against his fan belt. He squinted into his compactly built engine. "Is it? A good morning?"

I sat down on the curb and sipped my coffee. Nona Parker wanted to lose five pounds before next weekend. She'd gone back to bed to avoid the temptation of the kitchen. I'd made a full pot for myself. In Miz Hundy's camper, out at the barn, making coffee was also my job. Regardless of the stall or the horse, I always had a thermos nearby and my small tape player.

Nodding at the Volkswagen, I said, "What's wrong with her?"

"Cracked head. Your shoulder's back to normal then?"

"Good as new."

"Figured it was. Due to professional rivalry, however, I can't help double-checking another doc's work."

A ginger tabby climbed Mrs. Parker's front steps to snack on the dish I'd left for my own cat. Hadn't seen hide nor hair of Lou since he'd run off all those weeks ago, but I had the front and back porches and our landing in town covered. What was keeping Lila?

Dr. Kazloswki reached for his red thermos. "Can I top you off?"

"Your coffee wasn't very good the other night. I'll just stick with what I've got."

He unbuttoned the sleeves of his light blue shirt and folded them up his arms. A chilly day for October, but he wore no coat. He picked up a book from the street and shoved it at me. "Read that? Aloud, if you would?"

"I'm not even supposed to be talking to you, Dr. Kazlowski."

"K., my patients in Tacoma used to call me. I used to be known as Dr. K. That hasn't caught on down here. I've disconnected the leads to the carburetor. Read the part after that."

I squinted at the small type. "And the generator, Dr. K."

"Do you have a picture?"

I showed him the photograph. I asked him did he have the early type throttle cable return spring assembly?

"Keep talking dirty to me." His voice was muffled by the raised hood.

I stared at him. The guy was weird but so was half the world. "Detach the heater-flap cables."

The doctor replied the car had no heater.

"Oh, yeah, it does."

He hunched over his bumper. He said that many a cold crack of dawn in 1975 on his way to his surgery rotation he would have appreciated the heater working. It was the car's one flaw. He waved across the street. "I believe you're being summoned."

Lila's glare could have frosted my heart if I wasn't already cold clear through. "What's your problem?" I said. I opened my door on the truck and swung up behind the wheel. I got the heater going right off. Lila wanted to know what I'd been saying to the doctor. "Wouldn't you like to know." She had no choice but to climb up. I would have driven off without her.

"Did you bring cigarettes?" she asked.

"Where's your necklace?" I nodded at her bare neck. "You forgot Jesus."

"Give me a smoke and cut the lip, Gwen."

I told her I had two left. I wouldn't be able to get more till tonight when the high school girl I knew came on at 7-Eleven. "We'll smoke them after your interview," I said.

At the guardrail I pulled my wheel on the curb to turn around. This end of the street was crowded this morning. It would be half past eleven by the time we got out to the hatchery. I drove fast down Main and really opened up the throttle on the highway. In seconds it seemed Miz Hundy's white fences flew by. Then the spot my mom died. No skid marks, no dents in the sheer cliff. Bark was scraped off a fir tree. I had an eyeblink impression of it, and then it was behind me. I grabbed hold of my thoughts and said, you're not going there. We climbed and dropped elevation and pounded over the Elochoman River. You couldn't see it for the brush and trees but if we got out and put our ear to the pavement we'd probably hear it, faithfully, twenty-four hours a day, cutting its channel to the Columbia. I slowed for the turn up the hatchery road, overhung by big leaf maples, orange and gold. Fir grew thicker as we climbed and the road widened into a gravel parking lot. A low government building stood on the other side of the fierce little river. Some people might call it a big creek. A hand-painted sign informed us the bridge was under repair. I parked and we got out.

We crossed the bridge and entered the main building and found two men sitting at a table in a little side room next to a glass case that held maps and old fishing rods. They were eating sandwiches.

The older one had a few white hairs on his tanned head. His T-shirt was soaking wet. He stared at me and then Lila a beat too long. The younger one was less wet, bearded and friendlier-looking.

"Is the manager around?" I said.

The older man answered, "Who's asking?"

"They're all down spawning," the younger guy said. "It's our last week for Coho."

"And Dennis? He's down there too? And where exactly is down?"

"What business do you have with Dennis?" The older man frowned as he looked Lila up and down. I didn't blame him. In her short skirt and heels she looked like trouble for the salmon hatchery.

"You're not his father," I said. "I know Dennis's father. So what business is it of yours what we want with him?"

"He's down at the J pond," the other one said. "We'll be going down in a minute, we can show you."

I turned around to head out the door we'd just come in. "You couldn't possibly be Althea Pérez's daughter?" The older man stopped me cold.

I turned back and watched him drag his palm over his scalp, feeling around for a sparse hair to tug. "She used to live a few trailers down from my wife and me. With her baby. Wife's gone, I'm still there."

"Yeah, that's her mom," Lila said. "She's touchy about that topic."

"I'll be damned," the man said.

"Are you coming, Lila?"

I circled the building. That old fart knew my mother? He'd recognized her through me? My instinct was to seal off the past, but even as I walked by troughs filled with tiny, darting fish, whole dark schools of them, I thought of a hundred things to ask him. Did he remember my mother on nice days, sitting on our big deck, picking her guitar? Her big, capable hands and cowboy boots and how young she was? When I looked back to my earliest days crawling around her on that wooden deck, my fat knees picking up slivers, my mother always had a guitar in her hands.

Dennis's lanky figure was easy to spot at the end of the gravel road. I thought we were both high-tailing it down there, but when I turned I saw Lila wasn't with me.

As I approached, Dennis climbed out of the pond with a salmon clamped against his chest. The fish fought him hard but he held it in a frightening grip. I'd heard Dennis was tough in a fight. I saw why. He'd strangle the life out of you. He was up to his knuckles in the Coho's throat, which he laid on a platform they'd rigged. A man standing nearby, a short little guy in a blue windbreaker, raised his baseball bat and womped it down over the salmon's snout.

"God, damn, Pete. You almost got me."

The man lifted the bat again. He did better a second time. Another man climbed out of the pond. "Hold the tail up, son, or you'll lose eggs."

I knew right away this man was the manager, the Scott person we'd come to see. He was broader in the chest than Dennis, though not as tall. His head was bare, his brown hair touched with gray. He held his Coho as Dennis had, one arm choking its throat, the thumb of his other hand buried in the hole in its belly. The fish struggled, but these guys were professionals. The man in the windbreaker hoisted his bat. This time he hit the board and the man jumped back, barely holding onto his Coho.

"Sorry," said thin little windbreaker man.

"His aim's fine when he's sober," said the man I believed was the manager, hugging the fight out of his salmon as if it was his girlfriend.

Dennis shook eggs from his dead female into a bucket. He straightened up and glanced at his boss. "Yeah. When he's sober," he said, and threw the carcass into the back of a nearby pickup. "How often is he, though?"

Lila spoke from my elbow, making me jump. "Jesus, Mary and Joseph," she muttered. "Give me that bat."

She stepped forward and pried the bat from windbreaker man's hands and lifted her eyebrows at Scott, the manager. "Well?" she said crisply. "What are we waiting for? I'm Lila. I'm here for the job."

The man eyed the girl's striking legs in black nylons that so far hadn't suffered a run. She ground her heels deeper into the gravel and raised the bat over her head. The man shrugged and served up the head of his tiring Coho. I could hardly register the swiftness of Lila's movement. She smashed the female in the brain.

The man introduced himself. He told Lila if she could keep doing that she'd have a job for the rest of the day. He bent over, inserted his knife where his thumb had been and spilled eggs into Dennis's bucket. He shook out every single egg. "I don't want slime or water getting in here. Come on, now," he said to Dennis and the windbreaker man. "Bring me five males. Is this work you're interested in?" He gave Lila a doubtful look.

"I have great hand-eye coordination," she explained. "I'm a ballerina. When you study with a teacher like mine, Miss Lee, you learn to *fouetté* on a dime. You have to know exactly what each part of your body is doing at any given instant."

"Should I head off then?" I said, but Lila didn't reply, if in fact she heard. She was watching her new boss with shining eyes. She had seen approval in his face.

"It's just like with the human species," the man was telling her. "The males are always ready. They have to wait on the females to ripen up. We have to spawn them by hand to control the eggs. It's a damn shame. Hurry up, son," he called to Dennis, who was back, thigh-deep in the pond. "Males. Five. You're keeping this young lady waiting."

I headed back up the road to the work that waited for me.

I had stalls and more stalls to clean but I took a break in early afternoon to groom Red. The fat old mare was my favorite in the barn. Right in the middle of raking out her mane and tail I had to drop to one knee in the corner of her stall. Mrs. Parker's heavy breakfast stayed put, but I dry-heaved, my stomach contracting, retching and spitting up saliva. The old mare shifted and blew into my hair. Her lips plucked at my shirt. I wanted to tell her not to worry about me, but I would never lie to a creature I considered a friend.

Fourteen

Lila called her mom that night and said she needed her old Corolla. She explained about her new job. About spawning Coho and then it would be winter steelhead and after that something else and by late next summer, Chinook. In the meantime there was hatchery maintenance and cleaning to be done. If screens blocked up with twigs and leaves the alarm went off and her new boss got mad. Water meant life to the place. "The hatchery's way up the highway, Mom. As you know perfectly well, I need my car." Stepping out of my shower, I could hear Lila still arguing on the phone.

Mrs. Parker's little foot nudged the bedroom door open. She still wore her cleaning uniform, her brown tweed skirt and white blouse and white running shoes with white rolled-down socks. I hated these clothes and wished she'd change into her black dragon robe and slippers, the only clothes she owned that suited her.

"So—she wowed them out there today, it sounds like?"

I nodded, rubbing my wet hair. I had a lot of geometry homework to do, English and Spanish, another full day at the barn tomorrow. I had my own life to think about.

"Well, this is good, this is good," Mrs. Parker said. She'd chewed off her pink lipstick with dinner and her thin mouth nearly vanished into her heavy face.

"I need a cigarette, Mrs. Parker."

It took her a few seconds to answer. "We're getting along, aren't we, Gwen? Why would you say something like that?"

"Just being honest." I dropped her towel and she frowned. "Sorry." I snatched it up.

She fluttered her hand at me, her wedding ring long gone and none to take its place. "It's just . . . they're new. Couldn't you have used one of my old ones if you're going to drop it everywhere?"

I put my foot on the rug between our beds and straightened it, just so. "I didn't know you had old towels. I just took one off the shelf."

"Go on, finish."

"I'm done." I reached for my backpack.

Mrs. Parker picked up the towel off the end of my bed and began rubbing clumsily at my head. Her body smelled sour. Usually by now she'd taken her bath.

"I'm sorry, dear, I'm on edge. I'm hungry."

It was the weirdest sensation, her rubbing my head. "Don't take this wrong, but cigarettes keep a lady thin, my mother always said."

"Is that how you maintain your figure?"

"Are you giving me a compliment, Mrs. Parker?"

"I suppose she bought you your first pack?"

I opened my mouth to mention Edgar Fuentes, but swallowed that. His van was one big ashtray after we were done together on his mattress. I'd lie next to him, both of us naked, and reach over his shoulder to take the Marlboro from his mouth. "American cigarettes," he'd sigh, "American girls."

"You guys are all cozy in here." Lila pushed open the door with her foot. She had left her muddy shoes by the back door. Her beautiful angora sweater was ruined. A thousand dry cleans couldn't save her skirt. A run traveled the long distance from her ankle to the inside of her thigh.

"If you get your car back, honey, you could drive down for your chemo and blood draws yourself. You ought to mention that to your mother."

"You'll get better with the merge lanes, Mrs. Parker."

I felt the familiar churning in the pit of my stomach. All week I'd been feeling it in the morning. Getting sick in Red's stall this afternoon was a first, and the feeling had never come at night. I breathed carefully but the feeling grew urgent. I ran out of the room. First my head in the toilet, then my pork chop from dinner. Green peas floated in the water. I rocked back on my heels. I wanted to cry, but why start now?

Fingers scraped the bathroom door. On my feet, flush, smooth my hair.

"Is it the flu?" Lila regarded me sternly. "I can't share a room with you if you are germy."

Mrs. Parker sighed in the hall and said that it was going around. One of the ladies on her team had been out a full week. How she was going to make her mortgage was anybody's guess.

"If you're not better by Monday I'll give you a note for school, Gwen." The last thing she said before shutting her bedroom door was, "Lila, your dinner's in the oven."

We heard her TV. A lot of laughing. Some sitcom. Sometimes the idea of Lila and me overwhelmed Nona Parker and she shut her door like this and didn't come out till morning.

Back in our room I sat down on my bed and propped my math book open and read problem number one. Bisect a given angle. I groped around in my backpack for my compass. My hands shook.

"Shut the door, Lila. You're so dumb you'll never figure this out, so I'll tell you. I think I'm pregnant."

"You're so over in this town." She pressed her narrow back against the poster of the famous dancer she'd taped up before I got here and could put up something of my own.

I nodded. "That's about your speed, to say that."

"With that guy at the gas station?"

"I guess you think you're pretty special for adding two and two and getting four, Lila." I drew another half circle. "It's going to be a girl. I'm like my mom. She said when she was carrying me she knew."

"So you're sure?"

"I'm pretty late for my period."

"Have you been to a doctor?"

"That's the next step, yeah."

Her face had paled. She pressed her hands to her yellow scarf and shook her head. Kept shaking it, shaking it.

She lifted her toe shoes off the closet doorknob. Lifted her skirt and hooked her thumbs in her tights and pulled them down her legs. Dropped them in the tiny waste can under the dressing table. "I'm having nothing to do with you."

"You share a room with me."

"You're my cross to bear. That won't last forever. I'm getting out of here."

God, I needed a cigarette. Where did I put my car keys? Seven-Eleven was five minutes up Main. The girl I knew came on at ten. I got my coat and went out. The cold air cleared my head. At the end of the street fog lay in the field, a few shreds hung in our neighbors' trees. Pavement gleamed in the streetlights. Half were burned out, but even so, I could see the cat on the hood of my truck was Lou. I could see this without a doubt. His white fur glowed. He sat still, watching me, and when I got closer his eyes looked greenish, weird and spaced out. I grabbed him. "About time you showed up, you."

I could feel every bone in his body when I stuffed him inside my suede coat. He made tiny mewling sounds, from relief or rage, I couldn't tell. I held him to my chugging heart as I climbed back up the front steps.

He landed lightly on the clean kitchen floor and cringed in one spot, not moving. Whatever that meant. I poured him a bowl of milk and put it right under his face. He lapped it with the focused attention I remembered. I wanted to touch the pair of gray wings over his eyes, my mom used to call it his toupee, but I felt, one thing at a time. His pink tongue didn't stop till the milk was gone. I'd heard too much could give a cat the runs and that's all I'd need. I told him, more in a few minutes, after he'd digested. I wondered, as I looked him over, if he held anywhere in his fur the memory of my mom's hands. Did he remember her in his small cat brain? The way she'd scratch absentmindedly between his ears while she read the paper in the morning—starting with obituaries? Did he think those were her footsteps coming around the corner?

"Nope," I whispered, "that's the person you have to avoid." Then Lila was there. She saw the cat cringing, still rooted to his spot, and stopped. He took her in with his gold, vacant eyes.

"I can't help noticing you're limping, Lila."

"He can't stay here."

"It's a miracle he found his way back. No thanks to you. If you put him out, you're dead."

"You know I'm vulnerable to infection."

"Not from my cat, you're not."

The hard bottoms of her toe shoes banged the linoleum. She yanked open the fridge. "Chemo kills off my white cells and makes it difficult for my immune system to function, Gwen. Bacteria from that *cat* could get inside my catheter and into my blood—" She brushed her filthy sweater with her fingertips. "That cat carries all the germs of our town. Plus, he's ugly."

"You'll be likewise if you put him out again," I replied. "You won't have a face."

I explained that Lou liked windowsills and high places. He'd probably enjoy the shelf in our closet. He'd find somewhere quiet and out of the way to sleep, she'd better leave him alone.

Lila said, "What about kitty litter?"

"Under my bed," I said. My knees cracked as I bent down to open the drawer under the stove. I pulled out Mrs. Parker's roasting pan. I asked Lila again why she was limping.

"Something's wrong with my damned ankle." She swallowed a glass of orange juice and licked her lips. "It's because I'm practicing alone all the time. I need a barre, a mirror, and not to mention a teacher so she can check my turnout. I think I'm holding my weight incorrectly."

"Maybe you pulled something out at the hatchery today when you were showing off."

"They like me." She smiled.

"And Dennis drove you home," I said. "What a gent."

"I thought you were going to get cigarettes," she said.

"Why don't you water that?" I nodded at the fern in the middle of the table.

"You could ask our friend the doctor for advice." She put her glass under the faucet. "I'll come with you."

"What do you expect him to tell me?"

She dribbled water all over the fern's shriveling leaves, piddling along, where I would have just upended the glass. "He could tell you if you're actually...*you* know."

"I can buy a kit that'll do that."

"Fine. I'm just trying to help."

"You want to embarrass me in front of him."

Her glance was scornful. "Wait till the kids at school find out. You don't know what embarrassed is, Gwen."

Her toe shoes were loud on the living room floor. "He'd have a bandage for my ankle," she called.

I followed her in there, turned off the lamps and climbed onto the couch, pressing my face to the window. Mrs. Parker had turned the heat down low for the night. God, she was cheap. Fog had drifted down the street. You could hardly see the street now. I felt that we were butted up against water, that I could have pushed a rowboat off the front lawn and drifted peacefully to the stop sign. If only the world was like that, and when you'd hit bottom in every respect, things became magical when you needed them to.

"He's not home," I informed her. "The man has a life."

"He's working at the hospital."

"You know he has a girlfriend, Lila. All those nurses."

She didn't say anything for a second. She just stared at his dark little house. "Oh, shut up."

Fifteen

A big box arrived a few days later. Lila and I still walked separately. I got home from school first and found it on the front porch. It was addressed to her. I left it on the kitchen table. Inside was a white cowboy hat with green parrot feather in the brim. *Until your hair grows back* said the note. Lila said nothing more about her car.

Sixteen

Lewis and Clark, the explorers, had to endure a winter at Fort Clatsop across the river in Oregon, and boy did they complain in their journals. We were reading about it in history. The Clatsop Indians didn't wear enough clothes. They gouged the white men for a few roots and berries. Not to mention the rain that rotted their elk meat before they could haul it to camp. Those two easterners couldn't get back to St. Louis fast enough. I could understand that. Winter in this corner of the world meant rubber boots and raincoats and stepping carefully around puddles everywhere you turned. This winter, especially, the way rain fell from the sky you would have thought God had just invented it.

Our street's hard edges were softened by water drops caught in streetlights when I came out onto the front porch Wednesday night before Thanksgiving. I was on my way to tell Edgar Fuentes I was carrying his child and what did he think about it? Going down the front steps, I flipped up the hood on my raincoat—one I'd brought home from the barn. Mrs. Parker was in the tub. Lila was in the kitchen cutting a big piece of dead skin off the ball of her foot.

"Hold it right there," she'd said when I came in to grab my keys off the counter. "Where do you think you're going?

I showed her my butt.

The truck's defroster worked slow and I used my sleeve. I was glad my cat was warm under my bed. Winter was a hard time to be homeless. On top of the rain no one put food out. Months I'd been here and I couldn't tell you what the neighbors looked like. They ran from their trucks to their front porches and slammed their doors on the rain and anyone else's problems.

Edgar's gas station was dark. If you wanted to fill up after five, you had to cross the Cowlitz River into Kelso. Behind the pumps, though, the man's van windows showed light. I parked behind DQ and waited for the old Mustang with its fender dragging to clear out of the drive-through before I got out. A girl wiped a counter inside, her back to me.

I stepped over an orange extension cord and rapped on Edgar's side panel. The door popped open—was he expecting someone? and the smell of pot rolled out. Just what I wanted getting in my clothes.

The man blinked and ran a hand over the neat black hair on his long chin. In the other he pinched a tiny white cig. "What if I was the police, Edgar?" I pushed past him and climbed into his van.

"I'm carrying our daughter," I blurted. "If you had a mailbox I could have just sent a letter." I reached into my rain-

coat pocket. I'd had the sense to bring my own smokes.
The man was still crouched near his side door. He threw
his head back and eyed me, a little wildly. Then he leaned
and plopped hard onto his child-sized mattress, all he
could fit in here, near the rear doors.

"That's what you've come to say?"

"I don't know what to do," I said.

"There's nothing to do. You have it."

"Not if I don't want to."

"Sit." He patted the mattress and I shrugged and let my
weight carry me down. I pulled comics from under my butt
and gathered them up in a pile. I saw ladies on the covers
in tiny leather outfits cracking whips, but also Archie and
Spiderman.

"What," I said. "We live here together in your van and
raise it, you and me?"

"You've told someone?" He lay back in his tangled
sheets and squashed his joint between his thumb and finger. I used to enjoy having his dark eyes on me. I used to
feel important and noticed. Now it just bugged me.

"I told my friend Lila."

"How about a doctor?"

"Lila asked me the same thing. I'm moving on it."

He lifted his arms behind his head. "You walk by, you
never look at me. Night after night I lie here and wait for
you to come and explain."

"Maybe you ought to leave town, Edgar."

"It's a free country, kid, even for a brown-skinned high-
school dropout. I'm not going anywhere."

I spread my hand over my stomach. "I don't want her to
know you."

"You do want it then. Well, that's something."

"Wait till everyone finds out," I groaned, dropping my head into my hands. "I'm so over in this town."

"I was more attractive to you," he murmured, "when your mother wanted me. Oh, now you stand up to leave? You can't handle the truth?"

"Don't start with that."

"You've tried so hard to be nothing like her." He rolled over and pulled his overalls from his dirty clothes near his double doors. He pulled out his green hat and planted it down firmly on his head. He lay back down and grinned at me. The hat fell off, but he clutched it back onto his head and held it there with one hand.

"Do you mind not wearing that dumb thing, Edgar?"

He sighed, removed his hat and carefully folded it. He placed what was left of his joint between his lips. His dark hair was parted cleanly down the middle and waved down either side of his long, somber face.

"Edgar, do you ever look in the mirror? You're too old for me."

"That is your mother's cruel tongue, passed on to you, I suppose."

My throat closed like a fist. "We're not going to talk about her." Water pooled in the lenses of my glasses.

He took hold of my wrist and pulled me down beside him on the mattress. "Please," he murmured. "I'm not the one you want to blame." He was warm and I wanted to lie against his chest and let him rock me, but he was my old life. I pulled free and crawled away.

"She told me I had to quit seeing you," I murmured. "She wouldn't want me to do this. She wouldn't want me here with you. Even though she didn't like Nona Parker, she'd want me to live with her, I know she would."

"Oh? You're the obedient daughter now?" Edgar replied. "When did that happen, kid?" He'd been holding my wrist but he let go now and climbed up to the front of his van to open his glove box. He pulled out a plastic baggie of pot and sprinkled it carefully across a fresh rolling paper. He rolled joints with precision, you had to say that for him.

"Here." He bent to light it, inhaled and passed it over. "This will help."

"I'm pregnant. I shouldn't even be smoking Pall Malls."

He put the joint in his own mouth and closed his eyes to inhale. "Stay the night."

"You know I can't."

"Your mother wouldn't want you to have this child. We both know that. It would hurt her to see you turn out just like her."

I swallowed. "And what's that supposed to mean? I did this on purpose?"

He shook his head.

"I made you feel young, she said."

His eyes popped open. "What crap are you talking?"

"When she found out about us, that night she got so mad? She said that's all it was. You wanted to be young again."

"Wanted to be young again," he snorted and leaned back on his mattress with his fingers laced behind his head. "What is that saying? That's the pot calling the kettle black? That was *her* problem. Your mother couldn't see the future for looking at the past. I think that's why I found it so difficult to like her."

I nodded. "You thought she was bitter. She said that."

"What have we done, kid? What have we done?"

"You guys liked each other," I whispered. "You'd meet at the tavern."

"She frightened me, actually. But she was an old friend. Of course we met."

"She said you only got involved with ladies who were in no position to complain when you dumped them, Edgar. Married ladies and so forth."

"You are cruel. But then you are young, as you have pointed out. It's you who will run from me, kid, not the other way around."

"As if you're really going to stick around after this news."

"I'm like your father, is what you mean?" Edgar opened one eye, then the other.

I pushed to my feet. I had to stand with my head lowered, tall as I was. "She was planning to leave that summer," I said. "She looked down from Miz Hundy's stage and saw you two standing near the door. You'd been on the road forever. You probably weren't the cleanest guys in the room that night. But you were different. All hair and big, staring eyes. The next thing she knew she was pregnant with me."

"Yes," Edgar replied tiredly, "Nashville, Althea and her guitar. She'd bought her ticket and two stupid Mexicans ruined her plans." He smiled a tight little smile. "Don't insult me, kid, by suggesting this again."

I thought he was going to say more but he didn't, he just lay back and shut his eyes again, his joint burning in his fingers. I pushed out the Dodge door, mumbling goodnight. The girl inside DQ stared into space. She had no customers. I put up my hood in case she could see me and because it was still misting rain. I carried my daughter up the sidewalk into her fatherless future.

Seventeen

Mrs. Parker said she was losing her mind. One minute she couldn't find her roasting pan, the next it was on the rack in the oven. "How could that be?" she said, pushing our bedroom door open. "Did one of you girls find it for me?" She hovered in our doorway, careful not to infringe on our privacy.

Lila looked at me and I looked at her, a warning in my glance. Silence, and Mrs. Parker heaved and dropped her heavy shoulders, crimped the ends of her dark red hair, and shut the door.

"If she had any idea what you've been using her pan for," Lila hissed.

"I cleaned out the kitty litter, I promise you, Lila."

Miz Hundy joined us for Thanksgiving dinner, bringing a candle centerpiece entwined with cedar boughs. Mrs.

Parker wasn't in her healthy, lose weight frame of mind. She wanted to show off. Her turkey and gravy melted in your mouth. Her stuffing, fluffy, like you dream about. Then Thanksgiving was over like all the other days following days and school started again.

Dennis and Lila had fallen into a routine. He swung by to pick her up two afternoons a week and Saturday mornings. Any day I expected to hear he'd made a move on her. Sure, Connie Beller was his girlfriend and sure, Lila was recovering from a long illness and looked it. However, you could balance teacups on her cheekbones and her yellow silk scarf gave her a rakish air and she had those blue, startling eyes. Girls like Lila didn't grow on trees.

If he'd come up behind her when she was cleaning raceways and tried to kiss her, she had her own secret, then. She didn't mention him at all.

A week after our turkey dinner, the first Friday night of December, I drove out to the barn to braid manes and tails for the show at the fairgrounds in the morning. All day it had rained and it was supposed to turn to snow.

I was taking a coffee break when my boss ambled through the sliding outer door, her face flushed, like it always was before a big show. I happened to be standing outside Gallant's stall, sipping from my thermos, and she paused to look him over.

"He's got the legs of a supermodel, Gwen. I bet you he jumps big, big, big one day—and soon."

I nodded at the cig clamped in her mouth. "Can I bum one? What are you talking about, he'll jump big? Do you have something up your sleeve, Miz Hundy?"

I handed her back her name-brand cigarettes.

She looked at her watch. "The Beller girl's coming out

to put Isabella over some jumps, isn't she? She's fearless. She could master this horse."

"I could work with him, Miz Hundy."

"You have your hands full," the lady murmured. She picked up a bucket of brushes off the nearby chair and entered the horse's stall. Gallant shifted away from my boss, but other than that, ignored her.

"Shoveling manure," I said bitterly.

"Which I pay you handsomely for," she called over her shoulder.

"You don't think I'm fearless enough to ride him?" I felt a tremor in my belly as I said that, like an elbow in the ribs, a little watery movement like a flip of a fin. "Round one, you came out on the losing end," Miz Hundy said. When her curry comb touched the horse's powerful hindquarters, he trembled as if he was covered with flies. Under his deep chest his legs were slender and overly delicate, prone to injury.

"Connie's just getting the hang of Isabella," I said. "They make a good team."

"Well, we won't get this fellow in the ring overnight," Miz Hundy replied. "Connie looks lovely on any of my mounts."

My hair had grown nearly two inches since my mom died. Most days I wore it back in a yellow ribbon. Wind blew in the outer door and pulled pieces loose and I hardly got the hair back behind my ears and pieces were loose again. I missed my mom on late afternoons like this one, when it had rained the whole day and darkness breathed down my neck. I wanted to be sitting with her in our old kitchen with the door open and rain plonking into her planter on the other side of the screen. Even if she ignored me, if she was reading some magazine, I wanted to be near her. The way she'd go *hmm* or chuckle at something she was reading. "Do you know stress can make you fat? No, really. It releases a hormone in your blood, Gwen. It's amazing we're not walruses, you and me, lately."

I tried to stick close to Miz Hundy when I fell into these moods. She moved fast, always something on her mind. Like now.

She swept down the breezeway, leaving it up to me to close Gallant's stall door. She always forgot the little things. She bolted out of the tack room lugging a pad and calfskin jumping saddle. I grabbed the reins of the bridle to keep them from dragging.

"Bring the brushes," she ordered.

I caught up to her around the other side of the barn. Connie would put Isabella over a few low jumps, nothing too strenuous, getting ready for the morning. Connie's own horse, Agnes, was down for the count. Her bowed tendon hadn't healed a whit. Maybe it never would. I'd moved her around to the other side of the barn.

"I'm supposed to do that, Miz Hundy." I meant my boss wasn't supposed to have Isabella's hoof clamped between her knees and her sharp tool digging out dirt and sawdust.

"Pardon me for calling a spade a spade," Miz Hundy said, breathing hard, "but when you sing out here, and I've heard you, you sound like your damn mother."

Just like Red, her mother, Isabella was sensitive about her feet. You had to pick around her frog carefully. Miz Hundy was impatient and the horse flinched and the lady said, "Whoa, girl," and just kept talking. "Lost my Friday night regulars to a joint over in Kelso. My pedal steel and fiddle combo? They want to be near the interstate, get the trucker business."

Miz Hundy dropped one hoof and picked up another one. "Whoa, girl."

"Be gentle, Miz Hundy."

"You want to audition? How would Friday nights suit you? My sister tells me you play the guitar morning, noon, and night at her house. Might as well get paid for it."

"Mrs. Parker didn't tell me it bugged her."

"It doesn't . . . *bug* her. She simply reported to me that you're damned attached to the thing. Belonged to your mother, didn't it?"

Miz Hundy straightened up and slapped Isabella on her rump to move her out of her way. "Nona won't like the idea of you in my tavern. I don't mind saying that's half the appeal. She never sets foot in there. It hurts my feelings."

The lady swung the light jumping saddle onto the mare's back.

"I don't know, Miz Hundy, your barn keeps me awful busy."

"Think on it. I had two, three jobs when I was your age. It's the only way to get ahead, Gwen. Work harder than the next guy."

"But you said I work too much!"

A couple of girls had arrived with their mothers. We could hear them talking loudly outside the barn. Miz Hundy told me to tie Isabella in the arena, she'd be two minutes, and she went to show the girls the horses they'd be riding in the morning. Trailers would arrive at daybreak and men would load the horses and deliver them with their tack to the fairgrounds. Miz Hundy passed the expense on to these girls' mothers.

When I headed out to the arena a few minutes later, Miz Hundy was banging on one of the jumps to lower the boards. Isabella's reins were in the sawdust because she had her cell phone pressed to her ear. "Goddamn, Connie," she barked, "what did you let her do that for? Well, hurry, I have to get to my tavern at a decent hour." She folded the phone back into her chest pocket. "Her mother's still in Portland with Connie's Honda. Her brother's driving her out. *He's* on time, anyway." She nodded toward her gravel road. Dr. K. pushed his bicycle out of early December darkness. He parked against her hemlock, under the barn lights.

"You *know* him, Miz Hundy?"

"Honey, I know every serious drinker in town. He wants to buy his daughter a horse, says he doesn't have much money. I'll show him Agnes."

"Agnes?"

"If I can get her out of the barn, Connie won't be distracted as far as going to town on Gallant is concerned."

"But Agnes is injured."

"With what this Kazlowski fellow wants to spend, that's the best he's going to get."

The woman straightened the collar on her riding jacket. She groped around in her pockets and pulled out lipstick, then her smokes. "Did I get any on my teeth?" she said. I shook my head. She passed me the whole pack of cigs before I asked.

"You keep them. I'm trying to quit. Eh!" She waved at the man who lifted his hand in return. You would have thought her barn was on fire by the way my boss bolted from the arena. She took the doctor's arm and led him into her barn.

Isabella was the kind of horse you'd expect to find in Miz

Hundy's barn. Like Red in her day, she was beautiful and strong. She carried her rider well. She didn't appreciate being tied in the ring, though, and I was about to quit braiding the mane on the Appaloosa Sweetness and bring her in when I heard *put-put*.

I made it around the barn in time to see a red sports car pull cross-wise into all three student spots. Connie Beller popped out the passenger side. "OK, I'm late," she blurted and tugged her helmet firmly on her head, fumbling with the chin strap. "Don't read me a riot act. That's the last time I let Mother take my car shopping. Is my horse ready?"

"In the arena."

Her brother Arthur was behind the wheel with the dome light on, fixing his hair. I spun on my heel and returned to my work.

A few minutes later Arthur Beller hollered from the barn door, "Gwen Pérez, it's been too long! Has that old lady made you a feminist yet?" His voice echoed to the rafters.

"It's OK, Arthur, they won't bite." I motioned him to come in and he sidled down the breezeway and I offered him a Pall Mall over the half door, the only thing I had to give him. He looked thinner, and the skin around his pale blue eyes seemed tighter. He and his sister shared those eyes. That hadn't changed.

"You wouldn't believe what I paid for this jacket, and you can't trust dry cleaners," he replied, fending me off.

I struck a match. "This is a barn, Arthur. Worse smells could get into your jacket than Pall Mall smoke. What happened in Philadelphia? Why are you home?"

"Arthur?" Connie burst through the barn door. "What are you doing? You're supposed to drop me off and go right back home. I can catch a ride with Gwen or Miz Hundy."

"Isabella's in the ring, Connie," I said.

"Where's your boss?" she demanded.

"Check Agnes's stall."

"Where do you think I've been?"

I shrugged. "Then she's in her camper softening up a potential buyer for your horse with whiskey."

"What are you talking about?"

I can do two things at once. I was having this conversation with brother and sister through the open door of Sweetness's stall and pushing my thumb through a fresh bag of rubber bands. I began to separate the Appaloosa's tail into workable sections.

"You only bandaged one of my horse's front legs," Connie continued.

"Only one's injured," I said.

"Arthur?" She turned to her brother. "What are you waiting for? You're supposed to go home."

"See you, Gwen."

"Yep, Arthur."

I heard the *put-put* of the guy's pretty car. Connie turned back to me. "He has to maintain his flexibility," she said. "Mother doesn't tell him to practice so I have to. I'm the one calling back east to sort this mess out. Mother says she'll do it, she'll do it, and she goes shopping and the days pass."

A light rain was falling. I'd have to bring Isabella in if Connie wasn't going to ride her. If all she wanted to do was make a stink about the bandages on her own weak mount or ramble about her brother. I liked Arthur's violin playing, but the guy himself wasn't worth breaking a sweat over. That bad summer my mom kicked me out of our apartment, I lived with his family. Connie was mercifully at horse camp. I lasted two days in that house where I was afraid to look directly at anything for fear of breaking it.

I was leading Isabella from the arena when Miz Hundy and Dr. Kazlowski came out of her camper holding glasses and arguing loudly. "What's this?" she demanded. "What the hell are you doing, Gwen?"

"I don't think Connie wants to ride Isabella in the rain," I replied, and I left them standing there.

Connie showed up in a few minutes, on the breezeway side of Isabella's stall. She put her finger in her teeth and worked her riding glove loose. She pulled off her gloves finger by finger, like a queen. "Did you hear? I broke up with Dennis Bly. I'm not seeing him anymore."

I stopped rubbing down Isabella's front hock. "You what?"

"Everyone at school's been talking about it. Come out from under your rock, Gwen."

I felt lightheaded. My heart hammered in my ears. "Out of the way, please."

She didn't budge her polished boots. "I worry what your friend Lila Abernathy will do now. She is your friend, isn't she? You know people laugh at her for working at the hatchery? She thought she could steal Dennis from me!"

"I got her that job, Connie, and I think you know it."

"Sure, he flirts with her," Connie continued, "a bit, from what I've heard. Now that we broke up I can look at Dennis candidly, almost like a brother. He doesn't mean anything by it. Dennis is a . . . confused boy."

I turned away. "Who the hell is that speaking, Connie? Your mother?"

"No one in my family likes him."

"So? You have a snobby, stuck up family."

"Well, that's charity for you. They sure opened their door to you."

"I only stayed two days."

"Your loss."

"Are you going to tell me what happened, Connie, or just keep beating around the bush?"

"He knocked Mother's jade elephant from Nigeria off our end table in the living room. I told him to be more careful, so he picked up her crystal vase and tossed it in the air to spite me. He caught it, but that's not the point. He doesn't have the proper respect for my family."

Connie had hardly ventured into the rain, so her riding clothes were impeccable, her white shirt crisp, her polished boots clean. She twirled her crop in her hand. She looked lightyears beyond the rest of us saps who had to struggle through our days.

"Don't you feel sorry for Dennis, Connie? With no mom and that weird dad of his? Couldn't you cut him some slack?"

"You go out with him, Gwen. You're welcome to him."

"Gwen!" Miz Hundy called from across the barn. "Come here, Gwen!"

"You're being summoned," Connie snickered.

"Bring me cotton padding, Gwen!" Miz Hundy hollered.

"OK!" I screamed. "OK!" Even though she was closer to the tack room than I was.

"Don't ball up this horse's tail, Gwen," Connie called after me. "Leave it down. Tiny braids. You know how I like it. I hope it's warmer in the morning."

I found Miz Hundy squatting, feeling Agnes's tendon with her man-sized hands. The doctor leaned against the feed trough and watched.

"How many times have I told you to bandage both legs on a bowed tendon, Gwen?" she said.

I handed her a red stretchy bandage. "Connie already informed me I screwed up."

"I don't pay you to screw up."

"I don't think she wants to sell Agnes, Miz Hundy."

The lady drew the red bandage around the horse's knee joint. My own knees cracked as I bent to insert a safety pin.

We rewrapped the horse's other front leg, then Miz Hundy straightened up and swatted her wet thighs. "You've got to give Connie a ride home."

"My work isn't done, Ma'am."

"Don't be so damned conscientious. Christ Almighty. I don't suppose you can fit James in too?" She swung her head in the doctor's direction. "And you can put his bike in back? You have the pickup."

The man cleared his throat. "I can wait for you, Leslie. You can drop me home."

I slapped the little Arab's tight rump. "Are you going to buy this horse for your daughter?" I asked the man.

"He wants Gallant." Miz Hundy bent for the bucket of bandages, grinning.

"Gallant?" I muttered.

The doctor drained the last swallow from his glass. "Next time I come I'll bring a camera. Cynthia would look good mounted on him."

"He never won anything," I said. "He dislocated my fucking shoulder."

"That was before we whacked him, Gwen. The juice is out of him."

"Leslie's going to turn him into a jumper, she says."

"That's chancy. No guarantees, Doctor."

"Gwen?" Miz Hundy said sharply. "Knock it off."

"Miz Hundy? What's that in your pocket?"

"My revolver, Gwen, don't ask a silly question." She pulled it out and gazed at it.

Compact, plated with nickel, the words Smith and Wesson gouged into its short barrel.

"I've put down a dog or two with this over the years," she sighed, "back in the days when I had dogs. Those fools will be fighting in my tavern tonight, if I know them. Do you know how many glasses I lose on the average Friday night? I can't make another insurance claim. It must be the weather that has everyone climbing the damn walls. This'll settle 'em."

She put the revolver back in her riding jacket as carelessly as if it was an orange. Her pocket bulged and the handle stuck out.

"I brought a thermos of coffee, Miz Hundy. I'm staying out here till I finish all the manes and tails. You'll have to drive Connie home."

"What would I do without her, James?" she said fondly, slapping me in the middle of my back.

The hours passed. I finished Sweetness and moved on to the dapple-gray, Sir, his silver mane and tail pampered and feminine. I was combing Isabella's pretty, thick tail when a truck turned up Miz Hundy's road. It sounded like a truck. I heard a door slam. I didn't think too much about it, could have been anyone, but some of the lady's tack was pricey, so I hit stop on my tape player and went to see who it was.

Isabella's stall is on the opposite side of the barn from the outer door. I had just set her door ajar when the outer door rolled open. Dennis Bly touched his cap. "Evening."

"What the hell are you doing here? Connie left two, three hours ago."

I backed into Isabella's stall and swung the half door shut. The sill was wide enough for Dennis to lean on it comfortably. Isabella lifted her head and stared at the guy too. I could smell the pond on him. They were spawning winter steelhead, Lila had said. His flannel shirt was wet. He had no coat, and even for December the night was cold.

"Pretty horse."

"Uh huh. Isabella's too pretty for her own good."

"Oh. The one Connie rides." He nodded. "Mind?" He helped himself to the latch and entered the stall. A carved ivory salmon swung from his tanned neck as he bent to hit the play button on my little tape player. Johnny Cash began to moan again about the woman in the long black veil. I backed around Isabella and grasped her thick tail. I didn't lift my head from my work.

He chuckled, dangling a pink ribbon over my shoulder. "Connie's favorite color. She's got you trained, Pérez."

"I live to serve. What are you doing here?"

"I'm a free man, Pérez."

Isabella's fine black tail swept the ground. I ran the steel comb through it again and again. "Just coming from the hatchery?"

"Like you I keep long hours, Pérez."

"Hand me the needle and thread and quit calling me that. I know my name."

The pink ribbon drifted toward my boot. I felt him standing behind me. I felt him occupying space right behind me. He lifted my hair. I froze. What the hell was he doing?

"What?" he said softly and ran his fingers up and down my neck. "You never had anybody touch you here before?"

The leather of his gloves was smooth and warm against my skin. He took my shoulders and turned me around to face him. His tongue entered my mouth as if it had been there many times before. An electric charge shot up my back. I pushed him away, hard. His face closed like a door.

"What?" he said, backing up a step.

"You don't like me, Dennis. Have you perhaps forgotten? Remember that time in math you said I wasn't your kind of girl?"

"You're pouring cold water on my fire, Pérez."

"You're supposed to be hitting on Lila."

"Lila," he snorted. "Jesus, Pérez. Suddenly it's real crowded in here. There's you, me, this horse, and a girl with cancer."

He tore off his cap and lassoed me around my neck with one long arm and pulled me into the hall. I managed to shut Isabella's door with my foot. I had a fleeting image of her calm brown eyes. Be careful, they seemed to say. Then I was in the feed room in his lap. He began paying flattering attention to my mouth. His kissing didn't quit. Had he been storing it up for me? I'm the one who pulled free again and stood to look at him, unfinished business between us.

"To be honest," I said, trying to catch my breath, "I don't mind you're here and not with Lila, but in Lila's defense I have to say, she's in remission, and they're doing some apparently very cool stuff on her clinical trial. Down in Portland? You know this, Dennis."

"Not for long."

"Excuse me?"

"I have a feeling about her," he shrugged.

"A feeling about what?"

"How did my old lady die, Pérez? Cancer in her . . ." he paused and laid his black glove over his heart. "Right here," he said gently. "It's nothing you beat. Jesus, let's change the subject. In fact, let's quit talking."

His gold eyes lit the dark room like headlights. He grabbed my hand and kissed the back of it where I'd banged it in the stall door earlier. I ran my fingers through his hair. I was standing on a cliff. The tips of my boots were already over. I wanted to touch him everywhere.

"I want to undress you," he said. "Can I?" He reached for my buttons. I pushed him away. I took his belt and yanked him on his feet. At the same time I pulled down his zipper. I hated to put my hand where Connie had already been. I was pretty sure she'd already been here. But oh well.

We kissed each other sloppily. I had so little practice. I really didn't know how to do it. My mouth wasn't rich, pampered and lip-glossed like Connie's. I was hungry. So was he. He pulled his tongue out from between my teeth and put it in my ear. He held my neck firmly as he lifted goose bumps across my whole body.

"How about we go in my truck." He rubbed his mouth against my shoulder. "I've got a blanket."

I pulled him down to the concrete I hadn't swept of hay that afternoon (luckily). He groaned and I found the sound fascinating. I pulled his jeans down to his knees. He lifted his butt and I dragged his underwear off. His legs were bone and muscle. He'd worked hard in his life, I could see that. I rocked back on my heels, waiting to see if he'd get as big as Edgar Fuentes.

"What are you waiting for? God Almighty, don't stare. Let

me just . . . uh . . . put it into action and you can decide
for yourself how you like it."

He knelt down to kiss me. I turned my head. So. My
staring made him uncomfortable. I found this heartening.
He wasn't such a pro as all that. I wriggled free of his grasp
and stood up. The legs of my jeans were so wide I could
step out of them without taking off my boots.

"You aren't wearing underwear," he said, sounding surprised and strangely reverent.

I jerked my shirt tail free of his grasp. "You try wearing
girls' underwear. See how you like it." I put one boot on
either side of him and lowered myself to his chest.

"You keep staring at it," he nodded at his cock. "Have
you seen one before?"

"Hasn't everybody, Dennis?"

"I didn't know you had a boyfriend."

"Like I'm going to tell you anything, Dennis. You tell me
the details of your life. We could discuss moms. Not having them. I don't think you get along with your dad much.
We could start there. And there's always Connie. I've seen
her little pink bed. You couldn't sneeze in that bed. That's
where her mom wanted me to sleep that summer I lived
with them two seconds."

He sank back against the hay bale I'd broken open that
evening. "Christ, woman. Don't mention that female again."

"You still like her?" I made a move to get up. He caught
my wrist and held me fast. "Don't go."

"You two broke up."

"That's right. And a guy's equipment is really fine-
tuned. We're wasting time."

I grabbed him roughly and started rubbing my hand up
and down the length of him.

"Hey!" He gritted his teeth. "Easy! Could you go easy on me?"

"Right now I kind of want to hurt you, Dennis."

I put my lips over the little pink end of his cock. Edgar taught me to do that. Dennis moaned. "That's the ticket, Pérez."

I took him into my mouth. He tasted salty like the ocean. I worked on him a little more, feeling pleased to see he was growing longer again.

"I'm ready," I announced.

Next thing I knew his big hatchery fingers, leather gloves and all, were pushing in between my legs, feeling around, just like Edgar had done our first time together in my mom's bed. I wasn't going to think about that man.

"It might hurt," Dennis said, "how many times have you done it, Pérez?"

The whole thing took less time than with Edgar. Edgar liked to play around first. He liked to draw it out. This time I just sucked in a couple of breaths and Dennis was entering me and I felt proud like I always did that I could do this. There was nothing wrong with me.

"God, this is good. Is it good for you, Pérez?"

I could feel him bang up against the end of me. I wanted him to stop now, I hurt, but I didn't want him to think I couldn't handle him. Then he was trickling down the inside of my leg. He swung off. "I always come too fast when the girl's pretty," he muttered and pushed me down on the floor and buried his face between my legs. I fell in love with Dennis's tongue. I got to the place I was going and Dennis hissed, "God, you're making me hot, can we do it again? Gwen?"

I opened my eyes. Dennis squatted beside me, his hair

in his eyes. He needed a haircut. Didn't his dad ever look at his kid's hair? The ivory salmon hung between his dark nipples. I could see his ribs.

"Did Connie give you this?" I took the pretty little thing between the tips of my fingers. It was warm from his neck. The salmon had been carved mid-jump, its tail lifting it out of an imaginary river.

"Forget Connie. Can we do it again?"

"Give me a minute."

"No. Let's do it now." He crouched over me. He was hard as an iron pipe.

"Do you mind if I fucking breathe?" I shouted, and he jerked his head up and stared at me. "I can't breathe, Dennis."

Wordlessly, he rolled over and I climbed on him. I hooked my thumb in his necklace. She gave it to him. I knew it.

He moved his hands under my shirt. Who did he think he was that he could touch my belly, my secret, with his damned black gloves? I took his hands and pushed them onto the floor.

Afterward we lay under our clothes in ankle-deep hay. The night was too cold for this. Dennis suggested we move into his extra cab with plenty of room to shove the seats back, but I said no. Sadness had snuck up on me. I was staring at the rafters, thinking about my interview with Miz Hundy that summer I was fourteen, that bad summer. I had the want ad in my pocket that day my mom came into the kitchen and said, "You'll never guess who's back in town, honey!" I had liver going in one pan, onions in the other. "Who?"

"Your father's friend has returned from California."

I pulled out the folded newspaper and slapped it on the counter. "I have a job, Mom. I passed the interview."

She flopped into a chair and rubbed her eyes. "Hand me a beer, huh? You rode out there on your bike? Aren't you the independent one."

I forked over strips of liver. "Miz Hundy's a feminist, Mom. She wanted to hire a girl. Lots of girls applied, girls who ride out there. She hired me, though. *Me!*"

"Probably to piss me off. I used to sing at her tavern."

I got plates from the cupboard and scraped onions out of the pan. "She says I have fire in my eyes and she made me lift bales of hay to see how strong I was."

"Uh...Pérez?" Dennis hovered above me, his bangs in his eyes. He had a good body, no doubt about it. He probably worked all summer with no shirt on. His chest was tanned and hairier than I would have guessed. He was shivering, but paying no attention to it. "I have a question. Why won't you let me touch you?" He looked genuinely concerned.

I sat up too. My work boots were still laced and tied in double knots. I tugged my jeans out of loose hay.

"I'm pregnant, Dennis. I have a fat belly and I'm embarrassed about it."

He thought I was joking. I watched his face change, harden up, behind his long hair. "Jesus."

"Is not the father," I muttered.

"You *do* have a boyfriend."

I zipped my jeans and smoothed my shirt over my stomach and pushed my arms into my heavy coat, not heavy enough for a night like tonight. The rain had stopped. I couldn't hear it drumming on the barn roof. Had it turned to snow?

I lowered my back pockets to the hay, leaning over so

my elbows dug into the wear spots on my knees. "You don't even like me, Dennis. Why did you stop in here tonight?"

"Who is he?" Dennis reached for his own jeans. I'd been using them as a pillow just a second ago.

"I can't believe you were throwing a three-thousand-dollar vase around the Bellers' living room," I replied. "Is your brain fucked? Why don't you apologize? Connie will take you back."

"I never see you talking to guys at school."

"Have you been watching?"

He shrugged. "What do you think?"

"You know the gas station down the street from school? You know the Mexican who works there? Actually, he was born in Texas."

"Old for you, isn't he?" Dennis pushed his arm into his flannel shirt. He couldn't button it with his gloves on, so he left it open. The shirt was still wet and it stuck to him.

"If you ever see him wearing a stupid-looking green hat, I made it for him."

"I guess you like him a lot if you're carrying his baby." He squinted at me. "You hide it pretty well in your clothes."

I stared at the hole in the feed-room wall. Wonderful, fat Red used to kick at feeding time. Food meant that much to her. One of the first things I did when I started here was move her a few stalls away and break her of the habit with a kick chain.

"I don't know that I have a bunch of choices about keeping it, Dennis."

Outside in the breezeway all the mares had their heads up. Their brown eyes were curious and concerned. In the overhead lights I could see the intelligence in their eyes. I entered Isabella's stall to get my bucket of gear and tape player. She butted me with her nose. I told her good luck in the morning.

Dennis was still in the feed room, sitting on the hay where we'd done our first kissing. His wet clothes were getting to him now because he was hunched up tight, shivering.

"Coming, Dennis?"

He waved at me without turning around.

"I can't let you stay here. Do you know anything about Miz Hundy? She doesn't like guys like you. The kind that sneak around. She says she wants me to have a life but I don't think that means fooling around in here on her hay."

I leaned into the unfinished wall and blew smoke at the rafters. "Buy the girl something, Dennis. She needs new riding gloves."

"Actually, Pérez, I like my freedom."

I ran my hand up and down the rough stud two-by-four. "Is that what tonight was about? You exercising your freedom?"

"You're carrying some Joe's baby, Pérez. What do you care what tonight was about?"

"You sound disappointed."

"It'll pass, Pérez." Dennis stared at me from behind his dark hair. "It'll pass."

I held his gaze. "You'd make a good jumper," I said finally. "You'd be leggy enough with a dark coat that would have a natural shine. Stubborn, of course, but strong over jumps if someone could point you in the right direction. Are you going to spread this around school?"

"Kids are going to notice it sooner or later."

"I'd prefer later, Dennis."

"Old man's on a tear," he muttered.

"What?"

"Raising Cain tonight. Moon must be full. My manager says I can't sleep at the hatchery anymore. Figured a barn . . . hell, I'll sleep in the woods."

He put a forefinger into his left glove and worked it off his hand. With the glove hanging from his teeth he stood up and I saw a pale scar across his palm like an old path in the woods.

"Old man did that when I was twelve. Caught me playing with myself and slammed my hand on the stove. Said put my pecker away till I get married or he'd do it again. I've never been . . . intimate with Connie. Easy to throw a damned vase around. I used to play ball. I'll catch anything. A girl like Connie, on the other hand, I don't know about that. That's different." Dennis worked his fingers back into the tight leather. "You weren't my first. Don't get any ideas you were. I don't know why I'm telling you. I'm going to treat you bad, Pérez. I'll be up front about it."

It was late. I was so, so tired.

I worked Miz Hundy's camper key off my key chain and held it out to him. "You can stay tonight only, Dennis. Don't drink any of her whiskey. You make sure you're gone early."

"Will you be offended if I act like I don't know you at school?"

I sagged against the open door and thought of Lila at home in bed. "You're about what I deserve, Dennis."

I walked through the barn without a backward glance. The night had turned bitter. Outside, snow fell. Maybe we'd have a White Christmas, our first in my whole life. Snow fell into my hair, down my neck. My wipers scraped badly. I could hardly see.

Mrs. Parker knew to expect me late. I was at her sister's

barn, accounted for, so I pointed my truck away from town. I rolled down my window and let icy blasts of air numb my face while my feet stayed warm from the heater. I overshot the cemetery road and slammed on my brakes and my rear swung around, into the next lane, but the highway was deserted. There was no one to collide with, just me and the snow.

I'd seen Mr. Bly around town. Who hadn't? He was a gyppo logger. He worked alone clearing small, private holdings of fir and hemlock overlooked by Weyerhaueser. People said he stole timber across property lines, but nothing had been proven. He was tall and broad-shouldered and you could see where Dennis got his swinging stride, but his face was heavy-jawed and pale, whereas Dennis's bones were lean and sharp and he was dark like his mother, who died of breast cancer when we were all in elementary school.

I parked at the bottom of the road and got out. The wind hit me hard, tearing my yellow ribbon off my hair. My hair blinded me and I stuffed it as best I could into my coat collar, then bunched my collar tight with my free hand to hold in heat and hair. I pulled my mom's flashlight out from under the front seat. I had gloves somewhere in some raincoat. A hat would have been nice. My ears ached as if they'd been slapped before I was halfway up the steep road, following the flashlight beam. I used my sleeve like a glove but my exposed hand, clutching my collar, turned numb. Hemlock and fir lined the road, a wall of darkness.

At my mom's funeral, before everyone ran to the tavern for sliced ham and beer, the priest had said a few words. He said even though she wasn't Catholic my mom would be welcomed into the kingdom of heaven. I didn't believe in heaven, but I liked his inclusiveness. I didn't agree with him when he said we leave our problems behind with our bodies. When the priest said that my head wagged. None of us get off that easy. You have to straighten out your life while you're alive or you stick around and find a way to do it when you're dead, which is why I believe in ghosts.

I was at the top of the hill now. The climb had warmed me some, but not my hand holding my coat closed or my ears. I crossed frozen grass. My beam found the path and a few seconds later the split-rail fence appeared along the top of the cliff. Lights were on across the river, fuzzy yellow through the blowing snow. Their mill ran twenty-four hours a day, same as ours. The smell of pulp would normally be everywhere, but tonight the wind blew in the wrong direction. The river's slow bend north blocked the lights of my own town. If the night had been clear I would have seen hills under the moon. I backtracked along the path. Were the dead watching the bob of my light at this moment, wondering if they should approach? Come out, come out, all of you! What's it like? Do you feel things, the cold of your grave and loneliness? Do you know my mother, a blonde in a denim outfit? So it's true, you do live on?

I knew she was along this side somewhere, near a huge stone angel on the grave of some early mover and shaker from town. Then my light hit her plaque. The hole for flowers at the base of her stone had filled with snow. I pulled out a plastic rose. L.D. Parker had been here. I held it by its stem and touched my cheek. Sadness rolled into me like sleeping sickness. What the hell was I doing out here?

The snow was starting to stick now. I crouched into the frozen ground and rested my shoulder against her stone. I was wet and shivering, but I wanted to push myself further, come right up to the edge and look over. I felt nothing of her presence. Her body was underneath me, I knew that, but I felt no argument forming between us. She was good as gone.

Eighteen

My muddy boots and wet coat landed on the back porch, next to Lila's plywood cages. Smokes and keys from the pockets. The floorboards creaked in the quiet house. It was hard to be perfectly soundless in the bedroom, peeling off my wet clothes, knocking into the dresser. "Damn it," I muttered.

"Gwen?" In the darkness, fresh out of her dreams, Lila sounded appallingly innocent and newborn.

"Go back to sleep, Lila."

"You're home late."

All the time scrubbing my face in the bathroom and brushing my hair a hundred times (it's your best feature, honey, take care of it), I was deciding whether to tell Lila the truth. I spit toothpaste into the sink and thought, No, rinsed water and thought, Yes. Better to hear it from me than him.

I got into bed and just told her. I skipped the details. "We didn't plan it, Lila."

She was quiet while the earth continued to turn, moving us toward morning.

"Aren't you going to say anything, Lila?"

"Came to the barn for what?"

"You want me to spell it out?"

Her sharp intake of breath was just the beginning. I braced myself.

"He had sex with you?"

"Lila, don't read too much into it."

"You aren't even that pretty."

The covers wouldn't reach my chin. My arms folded into my body to get warm. I faced the wall. She riffled around in darkness behind me. Crying? She knocked something over on the nightstand.

"I thought he liked me."

"I'm sure he does like you."

"You know what I mean." She had a Kleenex now. She blew her nose loudly.

"I don't think he's ever going to let himself get tangled up with you, Lila. If you'll get outside your own head for a second and think back to elementary school, you'll remember how his mom died."

"I'm in remission."

I swallowed hard. "Yes. You are."

"Does he think I'm going to die or something?"

I threw back my covers.

"Where are you going?" Lila whispered.

Again floorboards creaked in the quiet house. On the back porch my bare feet entered wet boots, my arms heft-ed up the heavy suede coat and buttons resisted my fingers. Snow had drifted in as high as the bottom step, but the sky had cleared and between the moon and several inches of snow Mrs. Parker's backyard was a fairyland, more beautiful than I'd ever seen it.

A straight shot to the river. Being with Dennis tonight had got me in that raw place where I stuffed memories. My mother, my mother.

Nineteen

My mom couldn't figure out why Edgar Fuentes had returned. She chewed on it constantly during the early part of that summer.

"What would make him leave golden California for our crummy town?" she'd say, chewing it along with salad or meatloaf.

"I mean," she'd continue, "he says he's tired of roofing cheap little tract houses that cost more than our mansions on the bluff. He says we're spoiled, we don't know what overpriced is. I think there's more to the story, Gwen. A woman left somewhere, maybe a child. What do you think, honey?"

I'd put down my fork. These conversations always occurred at dinner. "You want to know what I think? He lives in a van and they have wheels, Mom. One day he's in Bakersfield, one day he's here."

"I'm going to invite him and L.D. over to dinner. "L.D.'ll sniff the truth out of him."

The two men shook hands in our living room. They were both short, but L.D. had a blond crewcut and he was paler than ever next to Edgar, like most men in town. He pumped Edgar's hand a good one. "I remember you, bud. Mexicans stick out around here."

"L.D., don't be an ass. Edgar was born in Lubbock."

"What's brought you back to town, bud?"

"Sit down, please," my mom insisted.

"How long you aim to stay?" L.D. plopped onto the couch. Edgar took the armchair. "What a sensible question. How long do I aim to stay." He wore cowboy boots with high heels and bits of silver on the toes. L.D. wore brown logger boots with the laces double knotted.

"Edgar doesn't make plans." My mom slapped a beer into her boyfriend's hand. "He pumps gas, he smokes dope. Red or white, Edgar?"

L.D. gave the Mexican the business with his small blue eyes. "Any ties anywhere? Wife, children? Or do you just blow around in that van like some Texas tumbleweed? Only you've got California plates? That's your van at the curb, unless I'm mistaken?"

"No girlfriend, no ties," Edgar said. "That's my van. Yes."

I climbed out my mom's bedroom window and sat on the fire escape. July had moved in with hot days and clear, cold nights. Not a day went by I didn't think about high school at the end of summer. I hoped to turn over a new leaf in ninth grade, but in my heart of hearts I knew I laughed too loud. I blew girls over with my big voice. I had no talent for chit chat. I drilled to the point, whereas girls at my school liked to mosey up to what they meant. I liked clear tasks. Miz Hundy gave me plenty at her barn, and I loved her for it.

My mom called me to dinner. We'd unscrewed the legs from the kitchen table and rolled it into the living room so the four of us could fit around it.

"You in contact with this kid's father?" L.D. gave Edgar a cagey glance. "Is that what you're doing here? You got news?"

"That's precisely what I've been wondering." My mom sipped her wine.

Edgar rolled his corn cob with his brown fingers to cover it thoroughly with salt. "I met Gustavo Pérez nearly twenty years ago. I haven't kept in touch, I'm afraid." He paused, holding his corn delicately with his fingertips. "Between us, though? Gustavo always got the girls."

"I don't like the way you watch her." L.D. nodded at me. "What are you looking at her for?"

"You don't like a lot of things." Edgar bit into his corn with clean, white teeth.

"Gwen doesn't have a boyfriend," my mother said. "She's in love with Leslie Hundy's show barn." She held her nose.

"That should make you happy." The look Edgar gave my mother was tinged with annoyance. "Horses over boys."

"You don't have the faintest idea what makes this woman happy, bud."

"I know women, Althea's a woman."

"You know women, eh?" L.D. squinted across the table at the dark-skinned man. "Babe, he knows women. How about that?"

"L.D.!" My mom pushed back her chair and stormed out

of the living room. I found her leaning against her planter box on our landing.

I tried to stick up for L.D. "He's jealous, Mom. Can you blame him?"

"You heard what Edgar said," my mother answered, staring down the street. "Gustavo got the girls. He got me."

I broke off a piece of mint and brushed my cheek. The long summer evening had cooled, stars were coming out.

"Men leave ladies behind sometimes, Mom. Kids are born. They grow up. It's just life."

A long minute passed. "L.D.'s right. The man's been looking at you."

I said nothing, just stared off where she was looking. I knew this street like the back of my hand.

"He's been looking at you," she repeated.

"Ladies?" Edgar opened the screen door. "Everything all right out here?"

Ninth grade passed, and tenth, I grew taller and my glasses thicker. I couldn't see into my own future. Turned sixteen last May and the Saturday Edgar came by our apartment I'd been digging post holes. I was so worn out I could hardly climb our back stairs. You couldn't get a machine into those trees on the north side of Miz Hundy's barn. When I suggested she log it off first, she shook her head. "Timber market's not right."

The man had dressed carefully in a black silk shirt and khakis. He stood on our landing with his hands in his pockets, as if he had all the time in the world for me to decide to let him come in.

"My mom took fried chicken to the sort yard," I said finally, stepping back. "She's not here."

"L.D. is a well-fed man."

I left the door open and returned to the kitchen counter to finish putting cold chicken on bread. "If you want a sandwich, help yourself."

I came out of my shower feeling better. My blisters had softened and popped in the hot water, my hair and skin were clean. Edgar waited on our couch. I knew he waited for me, I'd known it somehow all along. His black eyes were so calm, following me across the oak floor to my little closet. I came out with my comb.

"That's a pretty tiny bedroom," he murmured sleepily.

"You're talking? You live in a Dodge van."

"You should come and see me sometime," he said softly and patted the couch. "Come here, baby. You don't mind if I call you that?"

I don't remember moving, but I guess I did. I was on the couch beside him. His brown fingers went up and down my arm. He pushed down the strap on my tank top. My muscles were starting to tighten up again from the day I'd had. I pulled away.

"What do you think you're doing?" I said.

"Music would be nice." He drew up the knees of his pants before kneeling over my mom's records. His black hair seemed to absorb light.

Edgar moved around our living room, humming "Slowhand" with Conway Twitty. He walked right up to me and folded me into his arms. He took my hand and put it between his legs. "Don't be squeamish, kid." I pulled my hand away. He smiled into my eyes. My mother's bedroom was right there. He danced me backward through her door. I felt a little bolder in her room. She did this with L.D. all the time. All the time they were locked in here. He moaned when I touched him and licked my ear.

We did it in her bed. I bled maybe three drops and he asked me if I was sure this was my first time.

"Yeah," I said, rolling away from him, "it's my first time. I don't bleed for just anyone, I guess."

"You're crueler than your mother."

"No, not as desperate." I sat up. I felt sore but very alive, as if I'd had another shower, ice cold.

"Speaking of her, come on, get up. I have to wash her sheets. We can do this again if you want, only not here. Not in her bed."

I ran her sheets down the back stairs. While the washer rocked and rolled, I sat on her red plastic couch and thought about what had just happened. I felt as if I'd lost something, shed a part of myself and I'd had no chance to say goodbye. I had gained too, though. Nobody at school had a guy Edgar's age. Van and all, if my mother wanted him, he must have been worth having.

I found her Pall Malls up front and scrounged matches in the drawer of her workstation. When I came back upstairs the man was gone. His smell lingered, though.

I came to his van every Saturday night after that and after sex I'd sit on his engine box and he'd peel me an orange.

"So your water pump broke out on the interstate?" I said one night, taking pieces of orange, one by one. "Were you pissed off you didn't get to Alaska?"

"I'd never seen a place as beautiful as this little town. I told Gustavo I'd never go back to Texas."

"How long till you guys met my mom at the tavern?"

Edgar shrugged. He was pulling on his pants, doing up his belt. "A week, I guess. Maria, Gustavo's girl, had left us. She hitched up the interstate with someone who treated her well, I hope. Did you know Gustavo brought a girl with him?"

"He forgot Maria quick when he saw my mom?"

"Don't ask me why the bastard left, kid, I don't know why." He handed me another piece of orange.

"It was me. He didn't want a kid."

"No. I don't think so, exactly."

"Then be exact."

"Why do you and your mother assume I know? We were punks traveling around together. Why do I have to answer for him?"

I changed the subject. "Tell me about your girlfriends, then."

"Now that's a boring story." Edgar fell back on his mattress, still holding half the orange, and laid his arm up over his eyes.

"Am I the youngest?"

"Yeah, you're the youngest. I could get kinda hooked on young."

"I'm going to make you a hat."

"All you have to make me is happy," he murmured.

Sometimes during sex a bored, lost feeling came over me, as if I'd wandered into the wrong life. The man's hands on my face smelled harsh and antiseptic. Dirty clothes were in a pile by his double side doors. He'd shudder over me, roll off and wipe himself with the T-shirt he'd worn that day, then he'd crawl up front and pull an orange out of a plastic sack.

"Wash your hands before you peel that, please. Do you live on oranges?"

"I was going to ask you what you were thinking, just now. When we were, when I was coming."

The van got hot during sex, sweat rolled into my ear and down my back. "I hate your life, Edgar."

I'm not sure why I kept seeing him. I felt noticed when I was with him, I suppose. I enjoyed his attention. He was someone to talk to, someone my mom wanted. A lot of other girls were having sex. None of them good reasons by themselves, but they added up. Here it was August and one day L.D. Parker said, "How long are you going to pretend you don't know, Althea?" and she came home and swung her red purse at my head. "Fool! Sneak! You've made me a laughingstock!"

The Saturday she died she had appointments with two logger's wives in the morning and I like to think she had perm rods and foils on her mind, not her lousy daughter, when she swung back around that corner and her boyfriend's low-slung car flipped and soared from the grip of gravity. The hand of God waited when she landed, had been waiting, and she dropped hard into that hand.

Twenty

The last Friday before Christmas vacation I ambled down the side hall where Connie Beller had her locker. A crowd of girls stood around her as usual, but Connie was gazing over their heads, bored, talking to some football player grinning goofily at her. She didn't need much convincing to step away from him.

"Where'd you buy Dennis his necklace?" I said.

"What?" Her pale blue eyes opened and closed. The hall was crowded and loud, the mood electric. The prospect of two weeks' vacation had that effect on us.

"That salmon he wears is carved from ivory, is that right?" I said.

She glanced at the silver choker I wore, same as always. "What do you know about Dennis's necklace, anyway?"

"I've got Christmas presents to buy, Connie. I don't have

all day. Where do you get a piece of ivory like that? I'd like
a dragon, actually."

"Portland."

"Can you narrow it down?"

"One of the specialty shops Mother likes." She shrugged.
"Mother shops that city inside and out. I don't really remember. I bought it last year." She turned away, back to her
friends and her locker door papered with old pictures of
her horse.

Twenty-one

I tried to start a conversation with Lila before bed that night. All week she'd communicated by her body language her rage about Dennis and me. All week she'd had evidence it was a one-time thing. The guy was true to his word and ignored me.

"What are you going to give Mrs. Parker for Christmas?" I said, coming in from the bathroom and flopping down on my side of the room.

"If I was talking to you, Gwen, which I'm not, I'd say a dandruff shampoo and conditioner set. Haven't you noticed her problem?"

"Just because you're jealous of people with hair, don't be cold, Lila."

"Suddenly you're Mrs. Parker's best friend? Well, you're

going to need her. Wait till I tell her you've been lying to her from day one."

I waited a minute until I felt calmer, then I said, "You want to go down to Portland with me and look around, do some Christmas shopping?"

"Portland means one thing to me, Gwen, the hospital."

"Don't forget your mother. She lives there too."

"I do forget her, actually."

"And you're going to audition to get your ass on stage in Portland, so that's something else."

"Turn out the light, Gwen."

Twenty-two

We did have a White Christmas, the first I could remember. Lila gave me a handful of guitar picks. Mrs. Parker gave me a chunk of turquoise on a silver chain. I lifted it from its bed of cotton Christmas morning and just stared at it.

"It's not Jesus," I breathed, "there's no suffering body. Mrs. Parker, *thank* you."

"Guess what, Mrs. Parker," Lila murmured. "Gwen's pregnant." The complete set of Jesus's parables, in storybook form, was half unwrapped in her lap.

"You asshole." I sat back and waited.

Mrs. Parker sat perfectly still, as if deep in thought. Then she slammed her tiny hands over her ears. "No!"

"Oh yes," Lila said, pulling out one shiny storybook with

the Lamb of God on the cover after the other. "And the father's old enough to be Gwen's own father. He works at the gas station near high school."

"You're fucked, Lila."

"Merry Christmas, Gwen," the girl said.

"Girls," Mrs. Parker breathed. "No! You're fighting. That's all this is?"

Nona Parker had drawn her dark red hair back in a white headband that left her heavy face exposed. She was pale, her bare little mouth pressed in a grim line.

"Remember the last big horse show, Mrs. Parker?" I shifted on the sofa, dropped my head into my hands.

"The show a couple of weeks ago, at the fairgrounds? Dennis Bly came to the barn that night. Please don't tell your sister. You were asleep when I got home, you probably don't even remember. Lila's waited all this time to get me back. She thinks she owns him."

"Is he the boy who's gotten you into trouble?" The woman was all business now. "His father goes to my church!"

"Mrs. Parker," Lila said impatiently, "the father is Edgar Fuentes at the gas station."

Nona Parker worked herself forward in her chair so her Oriental slippers were flat on the floor. She pushed her pink sweater past her elbows.

"Have you seen a doctor, Gwen?"

"No, Gwen hasn't, Mrs. Parker. I've asked her that myself. I left a note on the man's door across the street, an S.O.S. asking him to help us find one. A baby doctor. I haven't heard back."

"You what?" I hollered.

"Gwen's got all this pride. She doesn't want Dr. Kazlowski to know her life is screwed up," Lila continued.

"Well, Gwen, you have to eat your pride. You have to own up to the fact you're carrying life."

Mrs. Parker picked her bright little earrings out of tissue paper and set them on the coffee table.

"I got them at Wal-Mart, Mrs. Parker," I said. "They're silver-plated only, I'm sorry. And they're horse heads, not dragons."

"I've always wanted children." The lady stared at her earrings, which seemed tackier now than they had in the store. "I can't have any of my own, and since I've known that my life has never been the same."

"We know, Mrs. Parker." Lila read the songs on the back of her Dolly Parton cassette. "That's why you take in kids like us."

"If I'd known you were going to get me on Christmas Day, Lila, you be staring at a sack of horse shit right now, all fancied up with ribbon."

I nodded at the earrings on the coffee table. "I hope you like them, Mrs. Parker?"

"She doesn't even have her ears pierced, Gwen. And that's right, just keep on swearing, digging yourself deeper."

"Gwen, you don't talk to boys. You don't have boys over. I fail to understand how something like this could happen."

"I'll move out," I mumbled. "This too shall pass."

"Is that what this man wants? Does he want you to move in with him?"

"Edgar lives in a van, for the thousandth time, Mrs. Parker!" Lila yelled.

"When are you due, honey?"

Before I could answer, Lila said, "May sometime."

"I guess I need to see a doctor to know for sure," I said.

"And you've been hiding this from me all this time? The entire time you've lived here?"

I nodded.

"What do you girls want for breakfast?" Mrs. Parker was on her feet now, slapping across the living room.

"That's it?" Lila bellowed. "You're done bawling her out?"

"Oh, I'll leave that for my sister."

We'd hardly started our pancakes and bacon before Mrs. Parker pushed back her chair. "I'm going to get dressed and call my sister right now."

"Right now?" I wailed, sitting on my hands to keep them from shaking.

"Yes, right now, and Gwen, I don't think you want to overhear our conversation."

"You mean you want me to go?"

"Well, not permanently. We don't want to send search dogs after you. I recommend you head into Ninth Street and get a jump on packing up dishes."

"It's Christmas!"

"It's my only day off, honey. I'll be over to help you."

Twenty-three

I was wrapping juice glasses when lizard-skin boots hit our back stairs. Miz Hundy didn't knock. After all, she owned the building. Her pale eyes held no warmth.

"I thought you had brains, you. I don't have words, I don't have words." She sat down hard in the slightly turned chair, the one I hadn't touched all these months, and put her head in her hands.

I swaddled our decorative plate of Washington State in newspaper. Over Seattle they'd painted a tiny jet, on the lower slopes of the mountains hung a red apple. Down the center of the plate and along its bottom they'd drawn a thick blue line for the Columbia, our river. My mom bought the plate at the fair one year, but never found the right place to hang it.

"I want you to get rid of it," Miz Hundy said grimly, lifting her head. "Nona says she'll never speak to me again if you do. Lift your shirt."

"I'm having it," I said stubbornly.

My boss got up so fast her chair hit the wall. She yanked my flannel shirt up and stared at my bare belly. "You've been hiding *this?*" She stared another second and turned away.

"I know it's Christmas, but you can't get this place cleaned out fast enough," she said. "I want to forget I ever knew your mother. You're her mess, but I'm the one left cleaning it up."

"This isn't her fault," I said, backing up to the wall.

"You and my sister get this emptied today and I'll put up a FOR RENT sign. As far as downstairs goes, I'll let Lonna have it. I won't have a Portland chain in here. Maybe I'll sell the building."

"I could run the shop."

"What's that?" She nodded at the tissue paper bundle on the table.

"It's your Christmas present, Miz Hundy," I said, blinking back tears. "Today *is* Christmas."

She pursed her lips, hesitated, then grabbed it and tucked it under her arm. "God damn you."

"Did you hear me, Miz Hundy? Let me run downstairs."

"And let you add high school dropout to single mother? Nona ought to run it, if we get down to it. Cleaning houses is wearing her out."

"What does she know about a beauty shop?"

"You're lippy for a foster kid, Gwen. Nona got her beautician's license before she was married. Why not my sister? She won't steal my heat all winter or use my washing machine for personal items."

"I could run it part-time."

"And pay me part-time rent?"

"Lonna won't last a month," I said bitterly. "Those ladies from the bluff have complicated blond heads, Miz Hundy. You let me do your hair. I'll prove I know what I'm talking about, except I'd blow your mind and make you brunette."

"Listen to her. You're fired from my barn."

"Miz Hundy!"

"You're a potential lawsuit, pushing a wheelbarrow around out there in my clay that gets so slick when it rains. I don't want you setting foot on my property."

I yanked open our cupboard above the toaster and pulled down half the stack of plates. My hands shook. Tears were not going to roll in front of her! Plenty of newspaper waited on the counter.

"I miss you already, Gwen," she sighed, her voice softening. "My barn misses you. Goodbye."

"Don't forget, extra grain for Red in the evening," I said. "You know what food means to her."

"It works against her in the ring, being so fat."

"Let the rest of your horses win ribbons, Miz Hundy." I blinked hard. The bad moment passed and I had no job. My heart beat in my chest. My hands kept wrapping dishes.

Twenty-four

$\mathcal{A}$ FOR RENT sign went up in the apartment that day, Christmas Day. Mrs. Parker taped it to the living room window so you could see it from Ninth Street. Goodwill would come for the velour couch and my mom's bed the following week, but everything else was in U-Haul boxes. That same day FOR RENT vanished from the window downstairs. The sign lay on the floor of Mrs. Parker's station wagon as we drove home.

"Does that mean Lonna's got the shop for sure?" I said.

"I won't allow white trash like her on my sister's property."

"That's what I am, Mrs. Parker, especially now. Sixteen and pregnant, right?"

"Your mother, not you."

I tipped my head into the cool window. We'd worked all day. I was beat. "Who's going to run the shop then?"

"Maybe I will," she mumbled, "maybe me."

We got KFC takeout and ate dinner in silence. Lila sauntered in, pale and fierce. "Aren't you guys just the coziest sight." She leaned over for a chicken thigh.

"You guys took long enough."

"Takes time to clean out a life." Mrs. Parker shrugged. "Now Gwen," she put her hand on my arm, "don't take it like that."

"Don't pay her any attention, Mrs. Parker. Gwen's a liar, she's sneaky."

"Dear, really, don't speak in that tone of voice."

I continued to tear chicken off the bone and said nothing. I mourned the loss of the barn, the apartment where I'd lived most of my life, my mom's beauty shop. Exhaustion lay on me like wet clothes.

"All this time pretending she was one thing, Mrs. Parker, when she was really another."

"Where in this house can I get peace?" Mrs. Parker sighed, heaving herself up for a napkin. She passed me one and we both wiped our mouths.

"I'm wondering the same thing," I said.

"I'll be in my room, girls, disturb me only if the house is on fire." The woman waddled down the hall carrying her plate.

I grabbed another breast from the box and followed Mrs. Parker down the hall. I shut the bedroom door with my foot.

The door popped right back open. "Are you avoiding me?" Lila said.

For once she wasn't wearing her toe shoes, but this didn't keep her from arranging her long bare feet in first position and swaying so her fingertips brushed the door.

"So you told Mrs. Parker I'm pregnant. Who's next? Kids at school?"

"You can't hide it from them much longer."

"Go ahead. It'll be your little moment on stage." I stuffed chicken skin into my mouth.

"Oh, I'll have lots more moments."

"No, you won't." I put down my plate and wiped my jeans. Something about the room didn't feel right.

"You don't think I'm going to make it as a ballerina?"

"You don't practice. You don't take lessons. You spend all your time at the hatchery." I got down on my knees and lifted the bedspread. No gold eyes. No cat.

"And who got me that job, I wonder?"

I checked the closet. "Where's Lou?"

Across the hall I scratched at Mrs. Parker's door and walked in through the smell of cheap perfume. "Don't mind me," I said, as she sat up and pulled her napkin out of her sweater and wiped her face. In the corner the TV flickered. I lifted her white fake-fur spread and found lots of sandals, snow boots and sneakers her fat feet had ruined, but no cat.

"I told you cats carry germs." Lila spoke from the hall. "If it makes you feel any better, he didn't want to go out. I had to drag him out. He scratched me."

She pushed up the sleeve of her angora sweater to show me long red marks in her pale arm.

"Lila, it's Christmas!"

"Merry Christmas," she murmured.

I ran for her. Kid in my belly and all, I knocked her into the hall and she hit the wall hard and fell and I grabbed her and shook her and her bald head banged the wall. She fell backward, all legs and yellow head, clutching her heart, her stupid catheter she thought would save her life. A million miles away Mrs. Parker was shouting, "Girls, girls!" Her big body moved between us. She was sobbing.

"Girls?" Lila gasped. "*Girls?* What are you talking about, Mrs. Parker? I had nothing to do with this! Kick her out. She's pregnant! She lied to you! She's . . . *violent*."

My anger went out of me. I sagged into Mrs. Parker's soft body and she let me go. We were both crying, her and me. I took off my glasses.

My coat and boots were on the back porch. Lila's green pumps were parked neatly between the washer and dryer, and I grabbed them too and dropped them in the hall. "Come on, Lila. We're going to go look for him."

"At this time of night, Gwen? It's Christmas," Mrs. Parker pleaded.

"Stay out of this," I replied. My cigarette calmed me down. The woman continued to look at me but no eye contact happened from my end.

After a minute Lila said, "Do you have an extra one of those?"

Handed her my pack.

"No," Mrs. Parker groaned, leaning into the wall and shaking her head. "Don't smoke. Please."

"Desperate circumstances, Mrs. Parker," Lila said in a clipped voice. "Gwen, what's lying on the ground outside? I haven't worn my pumps all week."

"Wear my rubbers then."

It was nearly nine o'clock, the ground was frozen. Lila's legs were bare and the rubber boots from the barn were too big for her. She was shivering before we'd made it to the sidewalk. The flashlight under the front seat was cold to my touch.

"We're walking, Lila."

She stopped with one leg hanging out the passenger side. "What the fuck?"

I came around and took her arm and started to pull her
up the sidewalk.

"Let go, damn you!"

I let her go. She was heavier than she looked, or else my
arms were just worn out from the day. "If you take off I'll
chase you down, Lila."

"You think you can run with that big belly?" she sneered.

"Try me."

The flashlight beam nosed under cars and porches,
under hedges, between houses, and flushed a few cats on
our way down to the guardrail but not a white one.

We passed Dr. Kazlowski's dark house and when we got
to the stop sign turned right.

"What makes you think he didn't go left?" she said.

I continued walking. Up and down Cherves, then
Colsom, Larkey and Spur. After that it was numbered
streets. It was Christmas night and Main was busy, everyone returning home after the big day. I'd lost a lot today:
my secret, my job at the barn, Miz Hundy's friendship, as
well as my mother's furniture and dishes and the memories those objects contained. Some day. Mrs. Parker's
turquoise hung from my neck, at least. And that meant
something.

At Fifth the flashlight kept going out, and banging it
against my leg didn't help. Was my cat under Mrs. Parker's
back porch, after all? I'd forgotten to look. Someone was
yelling at us across the street. A car had pulled to the
curb—a little car with a black top and Dr. Kazlowski's big
head hanging out the window.

"Ladies?" he said. "Can I offer you a lift?"

And then: "Today preferably, Gwen!" the man called, waving at me to hurry up. Lila was climbing into his front seat.

A break in traffic took nearly a minute, I sauntered over. He pulled a bag of groceries off the back seat to make room for me. Springs poked my butt. A little handle hung near my head and I grabbed it with both hands when he tromped the gas.

"You got it fixed," I said.

"I wised up and let the mechanics have at it."

"We're looking for a white cat," Lila said, trying to pull her belt on.

"It's jammed," the man said. "Has been for years."

"I let him out to breathe fresh air. Gwen thinks he doesn't know his way home. She's dragged me all around town looking for him."

While the car shuddered and idled at our one red light between the high school and Gilbert, the doctor turned to Lila and said, "I got your note, Miss Abernathy."

"My note that says big mouth behind us is pregnant? I left it over a week ago, Doctor."

The light changed.

"How come you call me Miss?" Lila smoothed down her scarf. "Like I'm some old lady?" Her fingers worked the knot loose at the base of her neck and pulled it tighter.

"First time you saw me, Doctor?" I said. "That night you were playing opera? Did you take one look at me and see pregnant written all over me? I was, even then. My daughter was inside me."

"She thinks she's having a girl," Lila scoffed.

He banged his front wheel into the curb in front of his house and popped out his door and I fumbled to move the seat lever to squeeze out.

"No, no, you girls don't. You come inside."

"You heard him, Gwen. We're coming inside."

"If you'd each grab a bag of groceries I'd be much obliged. Careful with the eggs. Leave the heavy stuff for me."

He meant the box of beer on the back seat.

My bag had potato chips and cookies and cans of something in the bottom. I left it on his counter and turned to beat it, but he said, "Whoa!" and held up his hands and pushed us back toward the living room. "Sit down," he said and pointed at his couch. He didn't rush off to make coffee like he did the last time. He didn't bring out his kitchen chair. He sat in his armchair and closed his eyes. He wore gold corduroy pants and a blue shirt, folded to his elbows.

"Whatever kind of day you've had, Dr. Kazlowski," I said, "it can't hold a candle to mine. There's a hot shower across the street with my name on it. If you get my drift?"

"What is it with you young ladies?" He dragged himself up straighter. "The way you bicker? It doesn't appear you have lives so easy you can squander each other. *You*, Miss Abernathy, have hardly given the slip to a serious illness—"

"The hell I haven't, Doctor! In March I'll be in remission one year."

"One year is nothing, Miss Abernathy."

"Funny," I murmured, "Dennis had the same concern."

Lila spun around. "*What* did Dennis say?"

The man dug a square of white cotton from his pocket. He pulled off his glasses.

"You're in remission, Miss Abernathy, and blessed be the saints, it's certainly better than the alternative. You're fortunate to be within driving distance of this hotshot researcher's clinical trial. I know him. I know what he's gambling with these low doses of chemotherapy over several months. He may be right. At any rate, the disease can return in the dead of night or the light of day or any damn time it pleases. Clinical trial or no clinical trial. Bickering with Gwen here seems a waste of your precious days. As for *you*—" the doctor swung his head my way, "I've got a whole litany of things to say to you, Gwen Pérez."

"Good, because no one else is saying anything to her," Lila muttered. "She gets pregnant and no one even bawls her out."

The man polished one lens then the other and pushed his wire frames back on his face. "Miss Abernathy. It's precisely those among us nobody's watching who are usually in deepest peril. I'm quite experienced with Gwen's type."

"Whatever that means, Doctor."

"All this because Dennis stopped at the barn one stupid night, Lila? Grow up."

"Who is this Dennis?"

"No you don't, Dr. Kazlowski. What about girls that are my type? What girls? What about them?" I leaned forward, all ears.

"Up in Tacoma." He tipped back his head and gazed at his ceiling. "In my other life. But the more things change the more they don't. Didn't I say I was going to avoid entanglement with you two?"

"I do have a doctor in mind," he continued. "I've just been to see her. Not solely on your account, Gwen, I must admit." The man groaned to his feet and wagged his head at his end table where he'd arranged a group of photos in gold frames. "My first wife."

"Your first wife!" Lila and I echoed.

He nodded at the photos. "I've got my wives arranged in chronological order. Gloria's on the left, in scrubs? I met her in anatomy class in 1973. She's holding the first baby she ever delivered."

Lila and I jumped all over ourselves to stare at the woman. The photo was dark and a little blurred. She had a round face, brown hair. She wasn't pretty. The pretty one was the blonde with red lipstick and pearls and a cream-colored sweater. "Wow," we said. Placed beside her, but slightly apart, was a larger photo of a girl about our age with intelligent blue eyes and strawberry blond bangs and the doctor's sharp nose and grave mouth.

The man was in the kitchen now, banging around. I waved the photo at him. "Your daughter who's getting the horse?"

"Duh, Gwen," Lila called.

"Are you going to buy her Gallant the ex-racehorse?"

"I quit the ER in June to go climbing. That'll be the end of my paycheck."

"In the mountains?"

"We'll just call you brain surgeon," Lila said.

I turned to her. "Do you want a knuckle sandwich?"

"Girls!" the man said. "Please." He opened a can of soup and poured it into a saucepan and filled the can with water. He opened drawers until he found a long wooden spoon.

"Didn't your wife give you dinner?" I said.

"We met at Denny's, very briefly. I drove an hour for a cup of coffee, I'm afraid."

"She's remarried." he added. "Therefore, if you must know, I'm dropping out, as they say, for as long as I can afford it. I need a rig. An RV. Something I can sleep in. I'll hit the Tetons in Wyoming if I can get there before the college kids, then up to British Columbia for the Bugaboos. Some of the best granite in Canada and it's a tad off the beaten track. I'm terrifically anti-social when I climb."

"Are you going to sell your car? Lila needs a car." I turned. "Right, Lila? Speak up. You've got your hatchery money."

"What about ballet lessons?"

"Huh?"

"I'm going to quit working at the hatchery and start dancing again."

"The hell you'll quit at the hatchery, Lila."

"Watch me."

"Girls, would it matter if I protested I've had a long day?" The doctor banged his spoon on his pot and opened his cupboard for sourdough bread.

"Come on, Lila, we'd better go."

"Hold it, Gwen," the man said, leaning against his counter and slurping soup from the pot. "Nine times out of ten an elementary school teacher can deliver a baby. However, it's that tenth time where an OB earns her money. The first Mrs. Kazlowski is Dr. Coleman now. As I said, happily remarried, apparently. She lives down the interstate in Vancouver, but runs a free clinic just next door to us, in Kelso. We'll have to match schedules. I'd like to go with you."

We said goodnight and beat it. Across the street I sat down on Mrs. Parker's front step and lit a smoke. I needed a breather.

"Can you spare one?" Lila said and I passed her the pack. Then: "He's sorted you out, anyway."

"Let's tell her we walked all the way over there, to Kelso, looking for my cat."

"She won't believe us."

"That's what took us so long, Lila, walking all the way to Kelso. Don't mention Kazlowski."

"How come he calls me Miss Abernathy?"

"Keep your voice down."

"If you do meet this wife, pick her brains, will you? See what she can tell you about him. He's weird."

I turned my head back and forth, looking for the glow of white fur under the streetlights. Every so often a truck turned in at the stop sign and nosed its way down the street to its share of the curb, a door slammed, someone shouted something to someone else.

I pushed my cig under my heel and tossed the butt in the direction of our bedroom window. It landed somewhere in the bushes.

"Come on, Lila. You'd better do the talking."

"Aw, I bet you she fell asleep."

Mrs. Parker waited in her living room, beneath her heavy crucifix. "Girls, we have to talk."

"About what, Mrs. Parker?" Lila was all innocence.

"Something has to change in this house."

"Do we fight that much, Mrs. Parker?" I said.

"Try constantly," Lila murmured.

"I'm tired," I said. "It's Christmas, Mrs. Parker. I'm going to take a shower and go to bed. Thank you for my necklace. I'll see you guys in the morning."

Twenty-five

Several days had passed. School would be up and running again in less than a week. Mrs. Parker was taking me to the poor people's clinic in the morning for an exam. Lucky me. Lila and I were passing our usual hour in our room before we washed our faces for bed.

"You won't be too mad at me if I tell the kids at school you're pregnant, right?" she said.

"Do you care if I'm mad, Lila?"

"Yeah, actually I do."

"No. I won't be too mad. They'll notice soon anyway."

"I guess it's a good thing I have leukemia." Lila picked up her magnifying glass to peer at her butterflies.

I lay on my back with my arms pillowing my head. "Run that by me again?"

"Illness protects me from doing stupid things."

"You mean like I've done?"

She straightened and turned. "I'm supposed to start growing hair any day now. It'll be my turn for a boyfriend."

"You're asking me for advice?"

She picked up the little alarm clock that would drag us awake as soon as school started and checked it against her watch.

"How do you get a boyfriend?"

"Do I currently have one, Lila? I'm hardly the one to ask. Ask Connie."

"She isn't seeing anyone full time. Not since Dennis." Lila gathered her syringe and bottles of antiseptic off the night table.

"You make it sound like Dennis is the love of her life. They never slept together, Lila."

"You're just saying that. Maybe you're trying to be nice." She glanced at me.

"Dennis is more like us than he's like Connie. He has problems, things about his life he wishes could change."

"You mean losing his mom? He's like us in that way?"

"You know that night he came to the barn? The night that's caused so much trouble? He was looking for a place to sleep, that's all."

Lila narrowed her eyes. "What are you talking about?"

"Don't you and Dennis talk while you're working together, Lila? Don't you know he doesn't get along with his father?"

"It's loud out there, Gwen, with all that running water. We talk. We talk about salmon."

"Lila?"

She paused in the doorway. "What?"

"The sooner you get him down off that pedestal the

better. I don't think you can see other boys until you pull the log called Dennis from your eye."

The tap went on in the bathroom. She was peeling off her bandage in front of the big mirror and flushing her catheter with heparin. Her hotshot doctor injected chemo through her tube and saved her veins. Eight more weeks and it would be March and she'd finish her clinical trial, and in her mind it would be goodbye catheter, hello life.

Twenty-six

Lila told a few girls I was pregnant and the news spread. I let her have her moment in the sun. For a day or so she was the center of attention. Every time I saw her yellow scarf in the halls, she had a crowd of girls around her. She looked flushed and happy. Even her old friend Connie Beller stopped at her locker to get the scoop. I walked by and the two of them were huddled there, whispering. I snapped a mental picture of them, one with healthy shining hair, the other's bald head wrapped stylishly away in yellow silk, and stored it away in my brain.

Sticks and stones can't hurt you, but guys jostled me or tried to grab my books. The linebacker from the back of math grabbed my shirt when I walked out the door. I shoved him and he shoved me into the building. Dennis showed up. "Leave her alone, Coover." The guy spun around. "Why? Sweet on her, Bly?" I took off for the woods.

Lunch followed math and that whole week I'd circle around to the south door to my locker and head for the woods with my paper sack. The weather had warmed up, the snow was gone.

We had another math test and I changed a few of Dennis's answers for old times' sake and wrote C- and passed it over my shoulder. He took it with his black glove and said nothing, not a word.

Days piled up on each other and were gone and who knew where time went. No complaining from me. Once my baby was born I'd get my own place, my own job, my own life. Not to say gratitude to Mrs. Parker didn't fill my heart.

Had a turn in detention before math even started one Wednesday, with January half gone. A Hank Williams lyric appeared across the corner of my desk.

weary blues from waitin'
Lord I've been waitin' too long

I pulled my arm back so Dennis could see. My teacher was right there, clearing her long throat, squatting down to see what I'd written. She wore a necklace of three curved pieces of silver.

"Just doing a little decorating." I shrugged.

She said speak to her after class.

Fifty minutes later I walked out of the empty classroom holding a slip of paper which required my presence in such-and-such classroom after school.

Dennis popped out of the woods and pulled me off the dirt path. "I want to talk to you."

"That makes one of us."

He pulled me under the trees. Mud gave way to drier ground, carpeted with needles. He pushed me up against a large fir.

"Lila quit at the hatchery." He spoke between clenched teeth. "You encouraged her, didn't you? You told her to quit?"

"She has this idea she's going to get on stage, Dennis." I was breathing hard. I'd missed him. At the same time fury whipped through me.

I knew it was coming. Saw it a mile off and did nothing to stop it. His lips were cold but he kissed me with the same care he'd used before. Weeks ago now, because time flew. His mouth was cold and his kiss thorough, and when he let go, the roots of my hair tingled. He took hold of my shirt and fumbled with my jeans.

He'd lost his mom young and no one, no one, had taught him to be gentle. He panicked and grabbed. I pushed him away.

"Hands off," I said.

"What," he rasped, "is wrong with you?"

"*Fuck* you, Dennis. That's all I have to say to you." Shoved off through dense branches.

"You love Fuentes, I guess?"

Spun around. "Yeah. You're so original."

"You wouldn't have his baby otherwise." Dennis had his ball cap off and the wind lifted his hair. "You wouldn't go through it. The way kids talk about you."

I stopped, took off my glasses and dragged my suede arm across my face, using the fringe to wipe my nose. Keeping my eyes open so no more water fell. "This damn school."

"Are you going to drop out?"

"I don't think Mrs. Parker or Miz Hundy will let me."

"They run your life?"

"They've been good to me."

"I heard the old lady fired you."

"What don't people talk about in this town, Dennis?"

"Well, back to me for a second? I'm trying to clean raceways, feed the babies, I have a million things to do and my boss has the flu. Why did Lila have to quit this week?"

"What pressing problems." I laughed. "Too bad I don't give a damn."

"I wish you did, Pérez."

"You like me, Dennis. I'm not Connie, though, so you've talked yourself out of it. So we both have private wishes. Oh, well."

"I'm trying to recover my reputation, Pérez."

"I thought one of the reasons you were popular at this stupid school, Dennis, was because you didn't care what people thought about you. You're Dennis Bly, the lone eagle. You quit cross-country to work at a salmon hatchery. You're from the wrong side of the tracks, but one of the most popular girls in school goes out with you."

"How did you work in a compliment there when you're telling me off?" He grinned.

"I feel sorry for you."

His dark eyes grew darker and I thought he was going to huff off all defensive, but he stayed his ground. He kicked at the base of the tree near him. "You're dangerous for a guy, Pérez."

I squared my shoulders against my own tree a few feet off.

"You're the whole package, you're the girl and the baby and the house all wrapped up in one."

"Most of life is scary, Dennis."

"I don't have your guts. Whatever you call it."

I shrugged.

"That was a compliment."

I shrugged a second time.

"The way kids talk about you." He shook his head.

"I can't believe you're afraid of them, Dennis. What's so special about your reputation, you're hanging on to it? Take off your stupid gloves. Let people see the scar."

"I shouldn't have showed you that."

"Oh, get fucked."

Now it was Dennis striding off through trees, throwing his arms up and plowing through wet branches. Well, let him go to all the work of being the one to leave the scene.

My mouth hurt from his kiss. Already I missed his physical presence, his intensity, and for that reason alone I waited to make sure I didn't catch up to him.

It was my teacher I almost knocked over when I stumbled back onto the path. "Oh!" she said, startled. She wore a thin jacket over her linen dress.

"What were you doing in there?" She gestured at the woods. "Students aren't allowed in there during lunch."

"Why do you think I like it in there?" I replied. "If you punish me, you have to get him too." I nodded down the hill, where Dennis was just pulling open the door of the main building.

Right in front of her I stepped back into the trees.

Twenty-seven

I saw Mrs. Kazlowski numero uno in February. On the appointed day I walked home from school and rang Dr. Kazlowski's doorbell. He peeled his eyeballs apart from his nap on his couch and climbed into my truck. He needed a shave, his hair flew around his ears, he looked as though he'd slept in his clothes, but hey. Beggars couldn't be snobs. I drove. The clinic was first come, first served and packed to the ceiling with ladies in maternity shirts, but I only had to wait an hour because of the man beside me, the only man in the waiting room.

When his wife entered the examining room I wouldn't have recognized her from her picture in Dr. Kazlowski's living room. The years had prettied her up quite a bit. She'd cut off her ponytail and poured a bottle of red wine over her brown hair. She wore a crisp white coat, low heels and a diamond ring the size of love itself. It flashed all over the place as we got acquainted. Then she pulled on latex gloves and pushed that ring inside my body. I held my breath, thought of the first time Edgar Fuentes entered me like this, in my mother's bed, but used him more as a launching point to jump to other thoughts. Was this lady with merlot-colored hair and knockout eyebrows the reason her ex-husband was in town? Was the man barking up her tree?

In her office afterward I received a cheery, "Dear, you've nearly finished your second trimester. You're fine, your child is fine. Do you know why you're here?"

I nodded. "Dr. Kazlowski wants you to rescue me from that yucky free clinic where Mrs. Parker took me. He wants you to be my doctor."

"He wants you to have an abortion."

I stared at her.

"James isn't good with touchy topics, dear. These conversations that are difficult, but necessary, he evades."

"Where is he?"

"This is a private meeting, Gwen. He's sitting outside."

"He wants me to have an abortion?"

"You're sixteen. Your life has hardly begun."

"This kid *is* my life, Dr. Coleman. Now, if you don't mind, my friend Lila and I want to know what kind of husband Dr. Kazlowski was. He drinks his soup from the pot, you know."

"I have no intention of wasting our precious time with such talk, dear."

I could tell she was frustrated with me, but this didn't keep her from smiling across her big important desk. She had even white teeth, the correct number for her mouth, not like her ex-husband who had big whistling gaps between his.

"Nearing the end of your second trimester, things can be tricky, but you're not considered late-term yet."

I rubbed the hump of my belly that was with me 24 hours a day. "You want to wipe her out?"

"You're asking me to enter complicated philosophical and some would say moral terrain, Gwen, when you say 'her'. I'm thinking of your best interests, you and only you."

Papers were scattered under her immaculate white elbows. She had a window behind her shoulder and one large picture on her desk. I thought about sticking my nose over to see who it was. I was pretty sure it wasn't Dr. Kazlowski.

"I'm having her, Dr. Coleman, so let's get the show on the road."

Her face was unreadable. "You're a young woman who knows her mind, anyway. You're underweight. In all other respects you're fine. I'm putting you on a regular schedule of appointments. This is against clinic rules, but I'll do it because James asked me to. If you wouldn't agree to an abortion."

"You failed, eh, Gloria?" Dr. Kazlowski hovered in the open doorway. He seemed big and raw next to this petite lady, too eager, on the verge of breaking something.

"This is a private meeting, James."

"You want me to have an abortion, Dr. Kazlowski?" I was on my feet, but he waved me back down in my chair and shut the door with his hiking boot. "If Gloria can't get you to see things sensibly, I don't know who can. I'm going to leave you in her capable hands on the off-chance I clear out before you deliver."

The lady doctor raised her eyebrows at him. "Why don't you simply make peace with your daughter, James? Life would be easier for all of us—for you, certainly, and for girls like Gwen you become involved with. You get their hopes up, James, and then you vanish." She turned to me. "He can be a hurricane, dear, I'm warning you. He'll blow into your life and blow right out."

"You're speaking from experience, I understand," I replied. "I won't ask for details."

She waved her hand dismissively. "What I'm saying is this. James will be off on his cockamamie climbing trip right about the time you deliver, Gwen. Don't come to rely on him."

"His trip sounds fun, Dr. Coleman."

"If he insists on rolling the dice on certain high-risk, solo climbs that's his business. I don't want you to worry about him." Light caught the woman's hair nicely as she bent and started gathering up papers.

"Gloria," Dr. Kazlowski. laughed, "I believe you still care about me. I'm profoundly flattered."

"This corner of the world doesn't see many truly talent-ed physicians, James, and you know it. What a shame to waste you." Her face shone with intelligence as she spoke.

Dr. Kazlowski winked at me. "Gloria's never trusted so much as a hill, or anything else above sea level, since Willi Unsoeld was killed in an avalanche on Mt. Rainier in 1979. One of the first Americans to summit Everest, you know, and I'm honored to say I was one of his philosophy stu-dents at Evergreen State College. You're right. Climbing *is* a roll of the dice. Not so different from marriage, eh?"

The doctor was reading papers in front of her intently and didn't reply.

"The year Unsoeld was killed, Gwen, she and I had been divorced long enough I'd given up on getting her back. I entered the holy state of matrimony a second time."

"James—"

"Dr. Coleman, do you know the mother of his daughter?" (Pick her brains, Lila had said.)

Up came her head. "You mean the woman with whom James entered the state of holy matrimony a fourth time?"

Dr. Coleman chuckled. "Actually, I do know her. As I said, though, Cynthia isn't speaking to her father. Hasn't for several years now."

I turned to Dr. Kazlowski, whose face and neck were red as a ripe tomato. "So the horse is a bribe? You're going to bribe your kid?"

He shrugged. "She's hardly a kid, she's nineteen."

"Cynthia was about your age, Gwen, when James left her mother," Dr. Coleman said helpfully.

"Do you want to know a fact about this woman?" Dr. Kazlowski nodded at the small, attractive lady behind the desk. "During our first year of residency, I came home from seventy-two hours without sleep to discover she'd moved out of our house into her epidemiology professor's condominium. She took our two dogs! She obviously wanted to continue her education on a more private basis!"

I nodded at Dr. Coleman's small hand, open on her desk. "He bought her that bad-ass diamond?"

"That tightwad? He wouldn't even allow the dogs to stay through the weekend. Gloria had the sense not to marry him. He wasn't particularly intelligent."

"Neither is the father of my baby," I said. "Which I'm having," I added darkly.

"James? Let's keep our dirty laundry in the hamper?" The

lady put her hands on her desk and pushed herself to her feet. "You see, Gwen, how quickly the man can waylay a conversation? If he wants to leave his carcass in the ice and snow of the Cascade Range this spring or summer, it is no concern of yours. You have problems of your own and I don't want you worrying about him."

Dr. Coleman came around her desk and folded her arms. Her pretty head reached her ex-husband's shoulder.

"Tell her, James," Dr. Coleman continued, "why your daughter isn't speaking to you."

Dr. Kazlowski shuffled toward the door. "I haven't touched a nurse since," he said. "Don't sharpen your knives on me too badly, ladies." There was a quality in his face, something troubled, and then he went out.

Twenty-eight

We were quiet on the drive home, the doctor and me. I thought he'd be bossy and insist on taking the wheel but he just sat with his knees up and didn't say a word. I failed to use my rearview mirror switching lanes over the Cowlitz River and almost side-swiped a guy. "Well, I've drawn up a will," he said in a mild voice and fell back into silence. February darkness had come down on us and the man continued gazing at his own reflection in his window and the yellow moons attached to steel poles that occasionally passed.

"You two sound like Lila and me, the way you argue," I said finally.

"She's my daughter's favorite, of all my wives. With the exception of her own mother, of course."

"The daughter who's not talking to you." I changed lanes as I entered our town.

"Speaking of that—people not talking to one another?" He cleared his throat. "You ought to pay Leslie Hundy a visit. She misses you, and if you don't see her fairly soon the feeling's going to harden in her, if you know what I mean."

"Actually, I don't have any idea, Doctor."

Upper Main Street was especially narrow with practically no shoulder. For my passenger's sake I kept an eye out for potholes, although I was missing a headlight and streetlights were few and far between. We passed a rusted-out warehouse and the lights of my old middle school. Above that the bluff glowed softly.

"You're more like Leslie Hundy than anyone in town, young lady."

"You don't even know her that well to say something like that."

"I'm one of her regulars. I think I do know her."

He asked me to let him off at the hospital. His shift started in twenty minutes. So I turned down Fifteenth to take the back way. Edgar Fuentes's van was parked behind the gas pumps, both building and van dark. A couple of kids stood at the counter inside DQ, their heads thrown back, eyeing the menu.

"When you finish climbing will you come back here, Dr. Kazlowski?"

"I don't want where I go to matter a lick to you, Gwen."

"Where will you go?"

"Any number of small towns, I should imagine. The big ERs up in Seattle and Tacoma prefer to hire docs who did their residencies in emergency medicine."

"Are you ever going to go back to your patients in Tacoma who called you Dr. K.?"

"Oh, most of them, I expect, are deceased. I don't really work in Infectious Disease anymore."

The lights of our tiny hospital appeared at the end of the block, a mass of bright lights. I coasted down a side street to get to the entrance to the emergency room and pulled to the curb. He made a move to get out. I grabbed his arm.

"No you don't. How did they die? Your patients?"

"Complications wrought by infection from HIV, mostly."

"They had AIDS?"

He hesitated. "Well, yes. I haven't mentioned that?"

"No, you haven't."

"That was a lifetime ago, Gwen. HIV treatments have improved dramatically in the past few years, but most of my patients, the ones I became most attached to, were profoundly noncompliant, so it didn't much matter, you see."

He stepped out, said "Good evening" and walked up the sidewalk into the lights of the hospital in his old pants and blue shirt, no coat as usual, his body nothing but a hanger for his clothes.

Twenty-nine

At dinner Mrs. Parker asked me how everything went. I told her fine. I was fine, my kid was fine.

"You like her then? This Dr. Coleman?"

"A lot."

"She's not one of those feminist types like my sister? Did she mention abortion?"

"Peas again, Mrs. Parker?" I said, cheerfully.

"She did suggest it, didn't she?" The woman slammed her sweet potato casserole onto the table and thudded toward the phone.

"The idea was Dr. Kazlowski's," I called. "He's at the hospital. I just dropped him off."

"Nearly finished with your second trimester," she muttered, clapping down the phone, "and they bring this up? What did you say?"

"I said no, Mrs. Parker."

"Well, thank goodness for that. You're not putting on enough weight. Did this doctor person say that?" She plopped bread by my elbow. "You've got to eat more."

"Could you grab butter while you're up?" I said. I'd have one slice to keep her off my back. "Dr. Kazlowski says I should go see your sister, Mrs. Parker."

"See her for what?"

"He says it's now or never. That I can somehow bring her around, but not to wait too long."

"She holds a grudge, that one. You disappointed her and I don't think she'll forgive you. My sister expects too much from a person. She talks about me? She's the one who can't abide a sinner. Only her definition of sin isn't the same as mine. I'm afraid of Leslie sometimes."

The bread tasted stale. Someone hadn't closed the bag tightly. I suspected Lila, sitting behind her plate, quiet as grass growing.

"Last fall she offered me a chance to sing at her tavern, Mrs. Parker. I'd like to take her up on that offer."

"Oh, you can't do that, Gwen. Not now when I'm just opening my own business."

"You have your own business already."

"Nobody cares what their cleaning lady does. A beauty shop is different. Needs to be respectable."

"So you are opening it?"

"If that bothers you, talk to my sister. She's the one who asked me to do it."

I buttered my bread and chewed and forced it down.

"Where are you going?" Mrs. Parker said.

"Down to my room to practice."

"You're on dishes," Lila said, breaking her silence.

"I'm aware of that."

"I got you permission to drive to school." Mrs. Parker smeared her pink mouth with her napkin. "A belly like yours, you shouldn't be walking. They gave me one of those stickers to put on your windshield?"

"Thank you, Mrs. Parker. Am I excused?"

The lady nodded. She wore her dark red hair pulled back in her white headband every day now. If she'd had Lila's cheekbones she would have been a knockout.

Lila looked up from her untouched casserole. "I'll forgive you, Gwen. If I can ride with you in the morning."

"If I find my cat, does he stay inside?"

She shrugged. "If I come down with an infection, you have to drive me to the hospital then."

"Lila, please," Mrs. Parker said. "Don't I take you down every month so they can poke and prod you? I'll do the driving if it comes to that. I don't want to hear another word about infection. You're inviting trouble."

Thirty

I went to see my old boss on Valentine's Day, don't ask me why. I thought about bringing her a card with a heart on it or some candy, but recovered my good sense and just brought my guitar. Valentines had passed back and forth all day at school and some girls, Connie Beller among them, even carried wilting red roses to class. I asked Lila what boy had given Connie her flowers and Lila said, don't worry, some football player. This made me happier than it should have, considering Dennis and I weren't speaking.

That Monday afternoon, though, I felt better than I had in weeks. I felt optimistic and eager to see my old boss again. I missed her raspy voice and cynicism and, of course, her barn. I parked behind our old apartment on Ninth Street. Happy Hour would be going strong, but Mondays were slow in the beer-drinking business.

The orange neon sign was lit in my mom's shop window. Nona Parker had a lady in the red chair. She was brushing color on her head. Her pink mouth fell open when she saw me and her little green eyes held a question. Did I approve? I kept my face neutral. My heart whacked in my chest and my legs moved. I would cross that bridge later.

The red door of the tavern was several more storefronts down the sidewalk. Inside, the room was dark and cool. A mirror hung behind the bar and bottles were stacked to the ceiling on wide plank shelves. The man leaning on the bar had a hefty mustache that partly hid his smile.

"We only book live acts on the weekends, sweetheart."

"Aren't you going to tell me I'm too young to be in here?" I said, keeping tight hold on my guitar.

"You're too young to be in here."

"Where's Miz Hundy?"

"You know who you look like?"

"Yes. Where's Miz Hundy?"

"I went to school with Althea Pérez. She used to sing here."

"And you want a medal?"

He frowned and pulled thoughtfully at his mustache. "L.H. is in her office." He waved toward the bare plywood stage. "Door's just behind the curtain. She's with her accountant, I warn you."

"L.H.?" I eyeballed the man curiously.

"Only behind her back," he chuckled. "Only behind her back."

I parted heavy black curtains on a door marked EMPLOYEES ONLY and stepped down into a hall with a concrete floor. The only lights were the ones coming out of the office halfway down. Fake paneling gave way to windows and Miz Hundy sat with her lizard-skin boots on her big, messy desk. A man in a dark suit sat on a low couch. Her eye moved to my face for an instant and then shifted back to him. I couldn't hear what he was telling her, but her eyes and mouth were grave.

One of those recent Nashville stars with a California body moaned on the jukebox. The singer was hitting the high notes, but she was all gloss and pop. I couldn't hear pedal steel or fiddle or any authentic instrument behind her voice.

Before the song was over Miz Hundy poked her head through her door. "I'm going to be a while, you."

She didn't keep me waiting all that long, but I'm the one who had to kick off the conversation. The lady greeted me with silence, her big hands folded on her desk.

(The accountant gave me one look and beat it.)

I was heartened, though, because across her hard man's chest a thoroughbred cleared a triple pole jump. The sweatshirt was my Christmas present.

"It's kind of a coincidence, you wearing that today, don't you think? You must have known I'd come to see you."

"Cut to the chase, you."

"You said I could sing for you some night, remember?"

"I made that offer months ago when I thought you had a brain in your head." She got up to pour coffee into a Styrofoam cup.

"Sounds like you're still mad." I tried to smile.

"Affirmative." She swallowed the coffee as if it was water.

"I'd like to explain, Miz Hundy."

She nodded at my guitar. "Hell. Go ahead, sing. It beats hearing your excuses. Between you and my accountant's gloom and doom. What a day." She shook her head. "I have to sell one of my horses, maybe two. Taxes, Gwen, the scourge of working people everywhere."

"How are your horses?" I said. "How's Red?"

"Getting fatter every day." She sat down in her hard chair and laced her hands behind her head. She had wet spots under her arms.

"Has she placed at any of the shows?"

"It's not really her fault, my best riders want Isabella or one of the younger mounts."

"Isn't Connie riding Isabella exclusively?"

"Girl has her hands full with Gallant." Miz Hundy raised her hand. "That's enough chit chat. I really haven't forgiven you for your stupidity—"

"Miz Hundy, please! Dr. Kazlowski told me to come."

"James worries about us not getting along? What a mother hen. Well, play me something, something soothing. I've got a headache."

A black-and-white photo of Elvis Presley hung on the wall above her brassy head. He looked so young and beautiful I wondered if he'd ever really existed.

"Gwen?" Miz Hundy snapped her boots down to the hard carpet. She made a move to get up but didn't. She stayed perched on the edge of her chair, as if her thoughts were too heavy to physically move.

"I don't know how to say this so I'll just say it. You're a responsibility I don't want."

"Dr. Kazlowski didn't lecture me at all. He took me to see his first wife, an OB."

"The man's used to trouble."

"Whatever that means."

"You're just a more attractive package than he typically encounters."

You mean AIDS?"

"Affirmative."

I frowned. "He and Dr. Coleman argue but I think they still like each other. She's remarried though. She has an awesome diamond ring. She's worried he's going to die on his climbing trip. He's going to climb a wall of ice on Mt. Rainier. I think she worries about him also because his daughter isn't talking to him."

"Isn't talking to him?" Miz Hundy said indignantly. "How is that possible? He's one of my favorite people in town."

"He was playing around on her mother, the fourth Mrs. Kazlowski," I explained.

"What else did this doctor gal tell you?"

"That he's working out his guilty feelings. That's why he gets involved with teenage girls like me."

"This doctor said that?"

"He is, isn't he?"

I waited for Miz Hundy to answer me, but she didn't. She was going to, but she caught herself with a shake of her head. "Whoa, whoa. We're getting sidetracked. I was saying . . . what was I saying? Your boyfriend, Edgar Fuentes—"

"He's not my boyfriend."

"Well, he's somebody's boyfriend. Men like him—men period—don't generally embrace the monastic lifestyle."

"He just lies around in his van and reads comics and gets stoned and when he hears the bell ding in Full Serve he rolls out to do his thing."

"Yes. And he forgets to check the air in my tires. I always have to ask."

"I think I know where you're going with this conversation, Miz Hundy, and I'm going to tell you right now, I'm raising my baby myself."

"Oh, are you now." She leaned over and poured the rest of the pot of coffee into her Styrofoam cup. Prints of her orange mouth were all around the top of it.

"Is someone sleeping in my camper, Gwen?"

"Oh, shit."

"Excuse me?"

I took a deep breath. "It's Dennis Bly, but I told him only one night. That was last December."

"Last December?"

"I never did get my key back. Uh . . . your key."

"Are you sleeping with him?" It was like a big unseen hand had passed winter over her face. She turned so cold.

"You invite all the boys to come out to my barn?" she said. "My barn is where you rendezvous? Did you copulate on my high-priced alfalfa?"

I backed up a few steps until I stood in the hall. "His dad burned him on the stove. He showed me the scar."

"Come again?"

"I'm speaking English, Miz Hundy. Mr. Bly, Dennis's father, burned him on the stove. He told him to put his pecker away till he got married—"

"No. I can't help the boy, if that's what you're asking."

I took off my glasses and blotted the water that trickled out of my eyes with my forearm.

"Oh, come on now."

"His father *burned* him, Miz Hundy."

She sat back in her chair and gave me a long, long look. "I don't share Bly's or my sister's view of the world. I'm no churchgoer. But I know something of the Good Book. The wise one told those ladies who wept for him to save it for themselves. They'd need it. I have to pass that advice along to you, kiddo. Save your tears."

"Can I have a cigarette, please?" I ran my sleeve across my face.

"When you're pregnant? Aw, the hell with it. James Kazlowski would be disappointed in me, but go ahead." Her bargain pack lay by her phone and she tossed it to me. Dug around under her papers for the lighter. The cig tasted incredible and came in the nick of time.

"Speaking of Mrs. Parker," I said (I was starting to recover now), "she's got my mom's shop up and running down the street."

"Look. I didn't rent to Lonna, I've heeded your wishes on that score. I don't want to hear a lot of complaining about this. Nona's back can't take many more years of washing bathtubs and people's crappers. I want better for her."

"Couldn't I help her?"

"I wasn't aware you enjoyed Nona's company to that extent, Gwen."

"Well, I pretty much lost yours."

"Oh, now—"

"In a couple of months I'll have a kid to support," I blurted. The woman looked so uncomfortable suddenly, I kept going. "I'm in no position to be picky, Miz Hundy. Besides, your sister's been good to me. I could work after school. Help her with inventory and clean-up. Maybe I could have a few customers of my own. You could be one of them. Two of Dr. Kazlowski's wives were brunettes. That's the color I have in mind for you."

She pulled her hand from her face. "You've still got the lip, I see."

"And there was one blonde and one Asian lady with black, black hair."

I got busy unbuckling my guitar. "Dr. Coleman's hair is

plum-colored now, but she was brunette in anatomy class when the doctor met her. It's not a crime if you like him, Miz Hundy. He's not that much younger than you. Something soothing, you said? A one, a two, a one, two, three, four . . . ."

Thirty-one

Lila had hair by March, soft yellow fuzz she kept touching with bewilderment. Yellow hair that deepened the blue of her eyes, if that was possible, and took the edge off her sharp cheekbones.

The first Friday night of the month, in honor of my performance at Miz Hundy's tavern, Lila solemnly folded her yellow scarf and put it away in her drawer. She and Mrs. Parker squeezed into my truck cab and even Waylon Jennings couldn't drown out their argument.

"I get my catheter out next week, Mrs. Parker. I am *too* ready to start seriously dancing."

"You get your doctor's permission, honey, we'll see."

I parked in the back lot of the beauty shop and left them to follow me or not. At a few minutes to nine I stood inside the tavern door with my guitar, leaning back to counterbalance the weight in my belly and to catch my breath. The place was hopping.

Miz Hundy banged through the double doors behind the bar and hopped onto her plywood stage. Everyone clapped. She wore a pink satin blouse and big grin.

"I got a treat for you tonight," she hollered through cupped hands. "You know I've wanted live music back in this place. Well, tonight, if you can read the sign out front, we got it. Some of you remember this kid's mother performing for me. Come on up here, Gwen Pérez!"

Heads turned and eyes, some of them bloodshot, peered at me from under baseball caps that advertised chainsaws and certain types of tractors. The men's faces were friendly, though. Miz Hundy had good live music. They trusted her.

I plowed up the center aisle, taking care not to bang heads with my hard-shell case, and the lady took my arm and hauled me up beside her, onto plywood that gave under my weight. "Give us a few minutes, folks, while we set up for her," she shouted.

An old Van Halen song filled the room. *Go ahead, jump.* Guys pushed back chairs and went to get more pitchers. Men surrounded the pool table.

Mrs. Parker and Lila hovered inside the plank door, looking for a spare seat. Pretty yellow-haired Lila, and even Mrs. Parker with her pink mouth and bright blue raincoat, looked out of place in this roomful of flannel shirts.

I yelled at them and waved. "Over here!"

"I could really get in trouble, having two high-school girls in here at once," Miz Hundy murmured. "You took liberties inviting that Abernathy girl."

I shouted them over and pointed to empty seats around behind stage, near the wall.

"We'll hardly see you," Mrs. Parker protested, taking off her plastic rain hat and patting her hair. She'd pinned the sides up with bobby pins and the rest of it had the mark of the curling iron.

"We know what she looks like, Mrs. Parker," Lila said, hanging her denim jacket on the back of one of the chairs and settling down to rest her chin in her slender hands. She stood out like a black eye. Already men at nearby tables were eyeing her.

They'd set up a folding chair for me and one mike for my guitar, one for my voice. The lights went down. The white light bathed me like the moon, my guitar felt good on my knees. I took off my glasses and cleaned off the smears with my shirt tail and stuffed my hair behind my ears. The small room had grown so quiet Miz Hundy's breathing was loud at the edge of stage. Salmon splashed upriver and people rolled and creaked in their graves on the cliff.

Someone coughed. "You heard Miz Hundy," I said, my voice loud in the quiet room. "My mom sang here when she was my age. She was nineteen when Gustavo Pérez walked in that door." I nodded at the red plank door and everyone turned to stare at it. It didn't open, it was just a door.

"And don't you know we'd already passed the hat to get her on the bus to Nashville?" a loud gravelly female voice said from the rear of the tavern. Lonna from above the Laundromat sat in the corner behind the pool table, a small woman with scrawny breasts and an orange pixie cut.

"Are you trying to say you dropped anything into that hat?" Mrs. Parker was on her feet at the corner of the stage, glaring across the smoky room. "Don't put on a show for this kid, trying to pretend you were her mother's friend."

"What are you doing out so late, Nona?" Lonna jabbed

the air with her cigarette. "You haven't wasted any time taking over Althea's business. I'll say that for you."

"At least we don't have mice running across our counters. We don't reuse our manicure sets, either."

"Nona, you don't even know how to give one."

"Are you going to let them get into a slugging match, Gwen? Or get busy singing?" Miz Hundy said calmly. She'd moved from the stage to her usual place behind the bar.

"You approve of the First Amendment, Leslie Hundy? The right of free expression? Let the women talk."

The voice belonged to Dr. Kazlowski. Where he'd been hiding was hard to say. Suddenly he was there, a few tables away from Lonna in the rear of the small, close room, lean and watchful, his Goretex jacket zipped to his chin. He raised his drink at me.

"Do you know anything by the first lady of country, Tammy Wynette? She's snug in my heart, along with Giuseppe Verdi."

"May she rest in peace," I replied, brushing my fingers over my strings. "She was married more times than you," I told him. "If my other doctor, Dr. Coleman, was here, I'd dedicate this song to her," and I poured "Stand By Your Man" into the microphone. I sang loud, just belted it out.

Sometimes it's hard to be a woman
Giving all your love to just one man

Miz Hundy stopped wiping down her bar to turn and stare at me. Several men lifted their heads off the pool table and eyed me from underneath their cap brims. Even Lila peeked around the corner. I knew what they all saw. A blond, tall, hunch-shouldered girl, almost seven months pregnant, a sign of the times, except I could sing. Around here that counted for something.

I moved into Conway Twitty's "Slowhand" because it has mattered to me since the night I lost my virginity to Edgar, and then I did a Dolly Parton song and one by EmmyLou Harris, then I figured I'd better get them on their feet.

"I'd like to dedicate this next song to the lady who hired me, Miz Hundy, and don't forget the *Miz.*"

Don't . . . don't step on my blue suede shoes . . .

A middle-aged lady came out on the little-cleared dance floor with a guy who had left high school maybe that minute. A few other couples scooted between tables, dancing with small, jerky movements. Over at the bar Miz Hundy drew her finger across her throat, so I rounded out my half-hour set with, "Thank you."

"Come on, you." She pinched my elbow in her claw. "Always leave them wanting more."

I mopped my face with my arm and followed her behind the curtain at the rear of the stage and down the concrete hall to her office, where she pulled a square of leather from the pocket of her shirt and laid a hundred-dollar bill in my hand.

"Put that in the bank for your college fund."

"My what?" I dropped onto the lady's couch and lifted my heavy, sweaty hair out of my face.

"Jesus if I know how you're going to get to college, just do as I say. Now. Your mother's boyfriend might be in. Just a head's up. L.D. comes in a lot these days, usually spoiling for a fight. I have to wave my piece at him."

"Loaded, Miz Hundy?"

"I'm just warning you, gal."

"He was my mom's boyfriend, he's not that important to me." I shrugged.

"Didn't say otherwise, gal, I'm just saying his ugly mug will be here. My former brother-in-law," Miz Hundy shook her head. "Your mother never married him. I have to say that for her."

"Is there anything else you wanted to say, Miz Hundy?"

"Besides it was a real pleasure watching you out there?" She lifted papers and dug around on her desk till she found her pack of smokes.

"L.D. wanted to go around to Fuentes's gas station with a shotgun," she continued, "after he heard about—you know. It took some diplomacy to talk him out of that idea. If you're bound and determined to have this child, Gwen, properly introduce me to its father."

"Roll down your window when Edgar's filling your Cadillac, Miz Hundy."

"What I mean is, how about dinner one of these Sunday nights? Both of you? Has to be Sunday, it's my only night off. I'll invite your friend, James Kazlowski."

"What for?"

"He's easy on the eyes. Does there have to be a what for? That hundred isn't for the lip."

Mrs. Parker was applying pink lipstick when I dropped into an empty chair at her table.

"Dear," she rubbed her lips, "you're very talented."

I tried to slap Lila's wrist, but she spun away out of reach and continued sipping Mrs. Parker's glass of beer.

"Is she supposed to be drinking that?" I said.

"You tell her. You try talking to her."

"You don't treat Lonna with kid gloves, Mrs. Parker, so don't do it with Lila."

"No," she said pleasantly, capping her lipstick. "I don't treat Lonna with kid gloves, that's right."

"Maybe we should let her work with us, Mrs. Parker."

"Who, Lonna?"

"Yes, Mrs. Parker. Lonna."

Lila pushed back her chair. "Don't mind me. I'm going to the bathroom."

"I have no talent as a beautician," Mrs. Parker sighed, crimping the ends of her hair in her fat hand. "I've had to return money to two ladies already and I've only been open a couple of weeks. I'm going to be the one working the phone and cleaning, honey. You'll have to do the rest. Is Lila going to take forever in the bathroom? If you're done singing, I think I'll go."

"Whoa, whoa, where's the fire?" Those words were followed by a whiff of piney cologne and I turned around to see my mother's old boyfriend, L.D. Parker, standing between the stage and our table. He had the same hard little blue eyes and blond buzz cut I remembered, and the same layer of fat over what was essentially the body of a bull.

"You two are leaving already?" the man said.

"I'm not, your former wife is." I nodded at Mrs. Parker.

"L.D., have you come to cause trouble?" the lady sighed, wriggling into her raincoat.

"Thanks for leaving the roses up at the cemetery, L.D.," I said, edging around him.

"What?"

"The roses, the plastic flowers? On my mom's grave?"

L.D. pawed at his patchy mustache. His little blue eyes looked sad. "I go up there every week."

I nodded at the lady buttoning up her raincoat beside us. "That's why she wanted to cremate her. Excuse me."

I dropped into an empty spot at the bar. It was after ten and the room had thinned out some. Dr. Kazlowski had most of the remaining females in the place sitting at a table with him near the center aisle. He was doing all the talking and every one of them was listening.

I ordered a Sprite so I could feel OK about lighting a cigarette. I heard a shout and turned around. Dr. Kazlowski's head lay on the table and beer rolled into his flyaway hair and ladies' laps and there were cries of "Oh! Oh!"

I was over there in a heartbeat and picked up the doctor's left arm in his nice maroon sweater. His arm was limp, heavy and bony and the wool soft as soft.

"He fell asleep," Lonna said. "That's all." The doctor's head had missed the ashtray and she continued using it for her cigarette. Her hair was so short her ears stuck out like a boy's. Why did she color it orange? Was this a mistake or an act of rebellion? It was a wonder she had any customers at all.

"How do you know, you?" Miz Hundy barked, who had also hopped to it from across the room.

"Too many nights in a row at the hospital." Lonna shrugged. "He was just telling us."

Dr. Kazlowski lifted his head, yawned and pulled off his glasses. "I had the strangest dream."

Ladies pushed back their chairs and marched toward the toilets with their beer-soaked laps and I dropped into one of their empty seats. Miz Hundy knelt down to pick up pieces of glass.

"I was in the hell of my residency again," Dr. Kazlowski continued. "I was in the OR with my first wife. I was on the table and she held the knife."

"Don't be pathetic, James, it's been twenty years." Miz Hundy straightened with her large hands full of broken glass. "There's plenty of other fish in the sea."

L.D. clapped her on the shoulder and she spun around. "God damn it, don't sneak up on me. You're usually earlier than this, L.D." In her lizard-skin boots, Miz Hundy was taller than he was.

"I'll take the girl home. Althea wouldn't want her here."

"Don't mention that name right now. I'm not in the mood." Miz Hundy pulled free of L.D. and moved toward the bar. Glass clattered into the trash can.

"You've gone too far, putting her on stage," L.D. called. "You ruined Althea and now you'll get the girl's hopes up!"

"Why didn't I go into a more lucrative area of medicine?" Dr. Kazlowski murmured, pushing back his chair and tugging me free of L.D. Parker's grip. "Come on," he said, "let's find a more peaceful corner."

He swung me across the floor to the far end of the bar and we collapsed onto stools. "Orthopedics, say?" he continued. "I could reef around on broken bones like those orthopods for a half million a year. But no, I had to become an internist, infectious disease at that, where my sub-specialty was treating the poor, the powerless, the noncompliant—patients I sought out, as Gloria never fails to remind me, out of ego and hubris as much as social conscience. And because she also said a change of pace would do me good, I'm locked into the salt mines of a small-town ER, stitching loggers back together."

"Bud? I'm taking the girl home." L.D. hovered behind us.

"Bartender, a double scotch for me and a soft drink for the young lady," Dr. Kazlowski said politely. "Bud?" He swiveled around to face the blond man. "Is that the correct terminology around here? No, bud, you're not."

"L.D., get back." Miz Hundy held her revolver carelessly. "You're smelling up my place with your damned cologne. It's all right, James, don't look so shocked. I enjoy the opportunity to use my piece."

"You enjoy it too much," L.D. whined, but he let go my arm.

"That's right. Now back up, L.D."

"Leslie," the doctor said. "Tell me that's not loaded."

"Farther, L.D.," Miz Hundy said, waving her piece at him. "I'm not filing another insurance claim, James." Only when L.D. had backed up between tables, all the way to the center aisle, did she lower her revolver. L.D. looked around, bewildered, and plunked into an available seat.

"Go on, Dr. Kazlowski," I hissed, "go talk to her."

"Me? She's holding a loaded weapon."

"Just make conversation. Calm her down. She likes you."

"Pérez?" I looked up, straight into a pair of gold eyeballs.

"Whole fucking town's popping up tonight," I said. "What are you doing here, Dennis?"

He smelled like fresh air. He wore his ball cap and a flannel shirt and black gloves, like always. He said to the logger on the stool beside me, "Could I convince you to move one over, mister?" And the guy said, "Don't see why not," and Dennis dropped onto the stool beside me, looking good, really good.

"Can you read the sign out front?" I said. "I went on at nine."

"I was out cleaning pens."

"Well, I guess they had to be cleaned tonight."

He leaned so close to me I could smell the soap he'd used in his shower. "It's called overtime, Pérez."

Dr. K. perked up. "Overtime at what, son? I know all about overtime."

"Salmon hatchery," Dennis replied and held out his hand. "I'm in Gwen's math class."

I pushed off my stool. "Excuse me."

Lila was giggling with some logger in the far corner of the room, over by the toilets, but Mrs. Parker was on it. Fully dressed in her raincoat, with plastic hat knotted under her fat chin, she thudded around tables toward Lila.

"You come here this instant! I'm taking you home!"

And then Dr. Kazlowski was right there murmuring "Home" in my ear, not letting me out of his sight, his gray hair long but thinning around his forehead.

"Home," he said quietly. "I am so profoundly tired. Can I catch a ride with you, sweetheart? I didn't want to be rude to any of those ladies nice enough to give me their company, but I'm exhausted."

"You fell asleep right in front of them and spilled beer on them," I said.

"But I was the one talking."

At the end of the bar Dennis sat with his back to us, two empty stools on his left. Hunched over a drink that didn't look like Coke. He leaned back and took a long swallow and wiped his mouth. My heart softened. I knew I should go over to him and say something, even just goodnight.

"Go on," the doctor murmured in my ear. "Go over to the boy. I'll wait."

"He doesn't talk to me at school. So he comes here tonight. So? I'm going to have a baby. I don't have time for this."

The doctor sighed. "Still, poor fellow."

Thirty-two

Three or four ladies offered to drive the doctor home, but he just wheeled his bike down the sidewalk without a word, heaved it in back of my truck, and climbed in after it. All the way down Main, Mrs. Parker and Lila and I were stone quiet in the front seat. Lila was in the doghouse for flirting with a man twice her age. This was a sensitive topic, of course.

On Gilbert Street I parked in my normal spot behind the station wagon. My belly slowed me down and Mrs. Parker was climbing her front steps by the time I got down from behind the wheel. "Hurry, girls," she said. "And you, Lila, especially you."

"Is Dr. Kazlowski OK?" Lila whispered to me.

"Narrow that down, Lila." I lowered my tailgate but the man didn't move in the bed of my truck.

"Did he drink too much?"

"I guess the first wife is the hardest one to drink out of your system," I replied cheerfully. "We're home, Doctor." I grabbed the man's hiking boot, but I might as well have grabbed a clump of grass and expected to move the earth. I took out one of my few remaining cigs and ducked down to light up out of the nosing, curious wind.

The night hadn't gone too badly and I felt kind of peaceful. For once it wasn't raining. Spring was weeks away, yet the air was soft.

Lila reached over and plucked the pack from my hand. "How come I always have to ask, Gwen?"

"Leaning against my truck she said shyly, "Yoo hoo, Dr. Kazlowski? Are you awake? I've got hair now. You might have noticed?"

"Mrs. Parker told you to hop to it," I reminded her.

The man groaned and sat up. "Of course I noticed, Miss Abernathy. I'm partial to blondes, you know."

"You are not," I murmured. "Three of your wives have dark hair, including *numero uno*, Dr. Coleman, my doctor. I hope tonight is the end of it. I hope you wake up tomorrow with her out of your system."

"I get my catheter removed next week, Doctor. So you were wrong. I *have* given the slip to leukemia."

"I'm a terrible bastard for implying otherwise."

"You had a point, though," I said. "You wanted us to quit fighting and appreciate each other."

"And are you? Appreciating each other?"

Neither one of us spoke right away.

"A man asked for her phone number tonight," I said finally, pulling hard on my Pall Mall. "He must have been forty. She's going to try to outdo me, Doctor, you watch."

"Really, Gwen—"

"The stars, girls. Look."

We all tipped back our heads and stared at the velvety sky.

"Are boys at school passé, then?" the doctor murmured, his head thrown back.

"They don't pay us any attention," Lila said.

"One of them was trying tonight."

"He's the worst," Lila said. I could feel her choosing her words carefully. "Dennis wants every girl he sees and none at all."

"I'll just say excuse me and go to bed," I said.

"See how jealous she gets when she's not the center of the conversation?" Lila snickered. "See?"

"You don't have to talk about me when I'm standing right here, Lila."

"We're arguing again, Dr. Kazlowski. You haven't said *your head, your head.* Are you getting used to us?"

"You're like my daughter's heavy metal music, I suppose," he replied. "I've acquired a tolerance for you." The man continued to stand behind my open tailgate, head thrown back, absorbing the wonder of the heavens.

"The daughter you haven't seen in how long? Excuse me." I elbowed him aside and slammed the back of my truck.

"There's nothing personal about death in the mountains, girls."

"We're talking about your daughter," Lila snapped.

"Drive to the Tetons by way of Ann Arbor, you mean? I suppose I could do that. She'll have some nasty and uncomfortable questions to ask me, questions about her mother and me. Questions for which I have no answers."

"Nurses." I let out a breath I hadn't realized I was holding. "Coming, Lila?"

"Your daughter is the only female you have in your life right now that would take you back, though, if I understand correctly?" Lila hadn't budged.

"Brutally honest is your middle name, I gather, Miss Abernathy?" The man sighed. "I don't remember . . . I don't seem . . . ah, there's my key."

"I've never seen you feel sorry for yourself, Dr. Kazlowski." I checked my pocket for my own set of keys.

"You don't know me well. I'm a champion at it."

"He's had too much to drink."

"No, Lila, he's just tired."

"Gwen Pérez, I hate to hear you defend a bastard like me."

"Gwen and I are going to learn to define ourselves in ways that don't include boys," Lila said.

"I'm going in," I said. "Goodnight."

"Thanks for the Tammy Wynette tonight!" the man shouted, his voice booming down the street.

Thirty-three

One week later we had another math test. Dennis didn't understand conic sections. What was new? I wrote a message across the bottom of his test. Lila's down in Portland today. Goodbye catheter. I thought you'd want to know.

He thumped me on the back and passed his test back, his handwriting so sloppy and tiny I had to stare at it for several seconds: Since we're on the subject of that female — buddy of mine wants to take her out.

I spun around. "Which buddy?" I hissed.

"Dennis, Gwen!" our teacher said.

Walking out of class, Dennis slowed down and fell back, into step with me. Football players and other kids swept past us. Someone bumped me. "Which buddy?" I said.

The lanky runner who sat across the aisle from Dennis

stopped in the dirt path and turned around to stare at us. Dennis nodded at him. "Dave Calhoun, that's who."

"Coming, Bly?" Calhoun shouted.

Dennis shrugged and started to walk off. I grabbed him. "I'm singing again tonight. Are you going to come?"

"You didn't seem thrilled by my appearance last Friday, Pérez. Think I'll pass."

"You came late. I was mad."

"Look, I'm not really in the mood, Pérez."

All the kids were at the bottom of the path now, filing into the main building, except for Dave Calhoun. Gangly like Dennis, wearing a ball cap and flannel shirt, he stood in the middle of the path with his hands in his pockets, waiting.

"Do your problems involve a girl?"

"Of course they involve a girl."

"So it's true what kids are saying? You're taking out that what's-her-name, Connie's friend?"

Dennis scuffed the ground with his boot. "Something about me, girls like to ask me out. I can't say no."

"Bly!" Dave Calhoun shouted.

"I have to go, Pérez."

"So—now you take out Connie's friends?"

"Everything that's different about you becomes annoying around here, Gwen. It was nice to see you at the tavern. It would have been nice if you'd talked to me. I'd had a long day too. I'm making my own life, and if you don't like that, I'm sorry."

"I changed a lot of answers for you in there, Dennis. Don't you know by now the tangent of an angle is sine over cosine?"

"You got me in math, Pérez, I'll give you that. But how's

that fact going to be useful to a guy making a career in fisheries management?" He turned and loped after his disappearing friend.

Thirty-four

Lila had plenty to crow about at dinner that night. "Hickman catheters are difficult to keep clean," she informed us. "Almost everybody gets an infection sooner or later from improper care or cleaning. I'm a rare exception. I didn't get a single infection in eight months. I'm nearly a first, my doctor says."

"Here's another first," I said, spearing French-cut beans. "You have an admirer."

Her eyes narrowed. "Are you teasing me?"

"Good heavens, dear." Mrs. Parker dabbed her little mouth with her napkin. "Gwen is giving you a compliment. You're lovely. You're both lovely girls."

"Dave Calhoun, the cross-country runner," I said. "Tight with Dennis?"

"I'm not interested." Lila fingered the ends of her yellow

hair. She had a good half inch now, with evidence, maybe, of natural curl and everything. "All of a sudden he likes me? I don't get it." She bit off the end of her hot dog.

Mrs. Parker was feeding us strange combinations lately, like string beans and hot dogs, broccoli and garlic bread.

"If nobody in this kitchen minds, I'm going to change the subject." Lila wiped her mouth. "Mrs. Parker, now that I'm rid of my catheter and I have my doctor's permission, it's time to begin dancing three afternoons a week and Saturdays. Gwen can drop me off after school, can't she?"

"You'll have to ask her, dear."

"*Make* her, Mrs. Parker."

Mrs. Parker pushed her red hair off her sweaty forehead and dabbed at her upper lip with her napkin. "Are you ready for such strenuous activity, Lila?"

"You're that attached to me, Mrs. Parker? You don't want to lose me to the bright lights of Portland?" Lila smiled.

"Oh, please." I went down the hall for my guitar.

Lila followed me. "Mondays, Wednesdays, and Fridays, Gwen. Those are the days I need rides."

I was standing in our closet. I pulled down the hat box and set it on my bed. "Can I wear this to my gig tonight?"

"I don't care."

"You should care, Lila, it's a present from your mom."

"I guess you know about Dennis and his new girl-friend?" Lila flopped onto her bed. "You eat lunch in the woods, but even you must have heard?"

I pushed the cowboy hat down on my blonde hair. The green feather in the brim gave me edge and style. "Do you have lipstick handy, Lila?"

"Connie says she doesn't want Dennis anymore," Lila continued, leaning over to open the drawer on the night table. "I don't know whether to believe her or not. She says she and Margaret Livesy are still friends. She says all she wants to do is jump that racehorse out at the barn."

I made my lips bright red and gave myself one final look in the mirror and picked up my guitar. "Dave Calhoun's in Connie's crowd."

"Don't you think I'm aware of that?" Lila pillowed her head with her folded arms. "If I went out with Dave, that's where I'd be, at her table again."

"Wish me luck tonight."

"With a voice like yours you don't need luck, Gwen."

Thirty-five

Miz Hundy had her dinner party for Edgar Fuentes, Dr. Kazlowski and me toward the end of March. I looked forward to it because I liked any excuse to spend time with her, but the whole idea of airing my dirty laundry in front of her embarrassed me. Edgar Fuentes embarrassed me, old enough to be my father, living in an old van that in my memory smelled of dope and sex.

On the appointed evening I got a spot right out front of the tavern. Miz Hundy's regulars were sitting at tables near the front windows, but the door I wanted was the unpainted one just to the right of her tavern door. Over seven months pregnant now, I was breathing hard by the time I reached the top of her inside staircase. Screwed into her apartment door was an iron knocker of a horse doing a nice little dressage move.

Miz Hundy opened before my knuckles hit wood. A

white V-necked blouse and long ruffled skirt softened her hard body. She took my arm and pulled me inside. "Doing all right?"

"Doing all right, Miz Hundy."

"You haven't been here since—"

"My mom's funeral, Miz Hundy."

"Any debilitating flashbacks?"

"I'll let you know, Miz Hundy."

Her living room was stuffed with pewter, American flags and old pine tables. Between the windows overlooking the sidewalk stood a hutch, heavy plank doors open on stacks of gold-rimmed china.

She pushed me down in a brown velvet armchair that matched nothing else in the room and gave me a glass of cranberry juice. "Why are men always late, Gwen?" Miz Hundy paced from wall to door and back. The sound of people laughing came through the floor.

"Let's prepare our game plan, eh? I'm going to offer Fuentes money to leave town. Agreed?"

"I've got five thousand dollars in the bank," I said, leaning forward eagerly.

"I'll sell a horse before I see you touch that money."

"I thought you had to sell one for taxes."

"No, I've just found a better accountant."

She refilled my cranberry juice even though I'd only taken two sips. We heard feet on the stairs. When the lady opened the door, Dr. Kazlowski stood there with his bicycle in his arms.

"You carried that up the steps? What kind of neighborhood do you think I live in, James? Put it there against the wall. Oh!" Miz Hundy said. "You've brought Fuentes with you—in your bike basket, James?"

"We met on the sidewalk," Dr. Kazlowski said cheerful-ly, wheeling his old ten-speed across the living room. He gave me a wink and spun around, his gray hair loose and flowing to his shoulders.

"Edgar, you've met Leslie Hundy?"

"This is my apartment, James, I'll conduct introductions."

Edgar's long face looked wary. He hung back near the door, his black eyes shifty.

Miz Hundy plucked at his hand and pumped hard. "If anything I say this evening gives you cardiac arrest, Fuentes, this man is a doctor."

"I've already told him. James Kazlowski." The doctor low-ered his head and shoulders in a gentlemanly bow.

Miz Hundy moved us all into her kitchen so she could keep an eye on her lasagna. Her oven wasn't working properly, she told us. Dinner would be a while yet.

She nodded us down into chairs at her long plank table. "In the meantime, we can get started," she said. "I'd like us to proceed in an orderly fashion. I have questions I'd like answered, Fuentes."

Edgar unzipped his leather jacket, but he didn't take it off. I could see his black silk shirt, neatly pressed. He had no iron or ironing board in his van that I was aware of, did he send out to the dry cleaner?

"You said this would be a friendly get-together, woman. I don't like you controlling everything."

"This probably won't be one of your top-ten great evenings, Fuentes. I'll warn you."

"That's not what you said when you invited me."

"I believe I attached a small warning label to my invita-tion, Fuentes, like the tobacco companies put on their cig-arette packs? I mentioned I'm Gwen Pérez's employer."

Edgar returned the woman's gaze. "You're not the only one who's fond of the kid."

Miz Hundy lifted her boot onto her chair and leaned on her thigh, staring all the while into Edgar's long face. "You're Mexican."

"I was born in Texas."

"Patriarchal culture, Mexico."

"You use big words." Edgar glanced at Dr. Kazlowski and back to the lean, tall lady hovering over him. "But I understand you're insulting me."

"We have an elephant in the room, Fuentes. Are you going to turn and look at her and say hello? Or do you feel too ashamed? We used to have laws to prevent what you did. As usual, the damned country isn't working right."

"Please, Miz Hundy—"

She waved me silent.

Edgar stretched his legs sideways out of his chair so his cowboy boots were in the middle of Miz Hundy's yellow linoleum floor. His boots were fancier than hers, with silver tips and a more canted heel.

"You're rude, woman, but that's all right. I'm here tonight because I've heard things about you and I'm curious to see if they're true. I didn't expect open arms so hey, I'm not offended. How the kid got pregnant, was that the question? I could answer that in two ways: the usual way, and how the hell do I know? The condom broke, I guess. I've made it to thirty-nine without becoming a father. I was proud of that."

"Why her? Why this one? Why not some other hapless teenager? Why my employee, Fuentes?"

"The kid's far from hapless," Edgar replied, "if I'm guessing the meaning of that word. Besides, who stopped me?

Has anyone in town run to the police? Have you, lady?"

Edgar's dark eyes flashed. An iciness I'd never seen before had come over his long face. He looked truly angry. I crossed my fingers under the table and hoped we got to the bribe soon.

"Just because we don't know how to defend our teenagers against interlopers like you, Fuentes . . . " Miz Hundy glanced at Dr. Kazlowski. "James, is he gloating?"

"I think he's scared shitless, Leslie. Excuse my language."

Edgar had his hand over his mouth but I could see his white teeth through his fingers. He was smiling. "You're the one afraid of her, man."

"What a terrible thing to say, Fuentes! James?"

Dr. Kazlowski refused to meet the lady's glance, scratching hard into his mass of gray hair instead. "I don't understand why this conversation has to be combative. It's an indisputable fact, fellow, you've impregnated a minor. Now, let's admit that and move on and figure out what to do next."

"Maybe having a child is the best thing that could happen to this kid. Maybe I've given her the gift of her life." Edgar tipped back in his chair, an insolent expression on his face.

"Set that chair down, Fuentes, this instant! You'll dig holes in my floor!"

"You really try to control everyone, don't you, lady?" Edgar snapped his chair obediently down to the yellow linoleum.

Dr. Kazlowski passed his hand over his face. "I think what this fellow is trying to say, Leslie, awkwardly, I'll grant you that, is that with Gwen under the large and protective wing you and your sister provide, she'll survive this ordeal. This experience will become part of the fabric of her life."

"Fabric of her life." Miz Hundy snorted. "No thanks to

you, James, leaving on this silly climbing trip . . . remind me when? Leaving the work to others."

"Who are better suited to it," the man murmured, dropping his gaze to the table. He pushed himself back in his chair and crossed his legs and kept his eyes on any part of the room but the face of the long-limbed woman staring him down.

Edgar leaned toward him and whispered, "She's a ball-breaker. Women. That's why I live on wheels."

"Was it charges of dope possession or trouble with a minor that drove you out of California, Fuentes?"

"I didn't rape the kid. Come on. So—I like women before they're really women. I've discovered when they're young they look up to you and what's wrong with that?"

Miz Hundy swung a bottle of red wine off the rack by her counter and twisted her corkscrew into it with jerky movements. She poured herself a glass and took a few long swallows, refilled it and swallowed again. Then she remembered her manners and filled glasses for her guests.

Edgar leaned over to pat my belly. "To the future," he said, lifting his wine glass in a toast. My hand batted his hand away and Cabernet splashed across his beige pants leg and the plank table.

Snickering, Miz Hundy tossed him a wet rag.

"How much money do you require to leave town, Fuentes?"

Edgar let his eye travel over Miz Hundy's body in her white ruffled blouse. "The problem with a bribe? You can't keep me from coming back."

"Forget it, Miz Hundy," I muttered, "give us free rent on the beauty shop while we get up and running instead."

"What," the lady said crisply, "are you talking about, you?"

I searched around in my pocket for a cigarette. "He just refused your bribe, Miz Hundy."

"I know the doctor there isn't going to say anything, but I will. Do you have to do that in front of me?" Miz Hundy snapped.

"They're ultra-lights. I'm hardly inhaling."

"I thought you wanted me to offer this fellow a bribe? I'm doing this for you. I don't give a damn what they are, put that out. I'm about to serve dinner."

I tamped out the stick in the woman's big glass ashtray in the center of her sturdy table.

"Take a good look at Miz Hundy's hair, Dr. Kazlowski," I murmured. "She's going to be brunette if I have to strap her down in my mother's red chair myself."

"I think she's rather nice as a blonde."

"So, Fuentes?" Miz Hundy said. "Where do we stand? Are you prepared to do half the work to raise this child?"

Edgar zipped up his jacket. "You know perfectly well, Leslie, may I call you Leslie? You're going to do everything you can to keep me away from the child."

"You see, Fuentes, that's where you're wrong." Miz Hundy leaned over and snatched up my partly-smoked cigarette. She held out her hand and I passed her my matches.

"If you refuse a bribe, what can I do? If you won't leave this town, which I more or less run, by the way, I'll find a way to make peace with you. I'll put you to good use. I'm excellent at cutting my losses."

Edgar took my chin in his hand and kissed me on the mouth. "I'm going," he said.

I started to wipe off his kiss but then I changed my mind. What the hell. He was my kid's father.

Plates of lasagna banged onto the table as Edgar crossed

the living room. The voices got louder downstairs, or maybe it was just there was dead silence in the kitchen. The lower door banged.

"I wasn't half rude enough, James. I wasn't half rude enough to that man. Does he always grab you like that?" Her eyes bored into me.

Dr. Kazlowski shoveled melted mozzarella and ricotta into his mouth and grabbed his wine. "You'll keep us all safe, Leslie, somehow."

The woman jabbed her cigarette at my plate. "Eat."

Thirty-six

Even Lila didn't dance on Sundays. She took a day of rest. When I returned home from Miz Hundy's with a Tupperware container of lasagna, she was lying on her bed with her head on her arm, reading a large book with butterflies on the cover. Dr. Kazlowski was still drinking wine with Miz Hundy, as far as I knew.

"Well? How'd it go?"

"Inconclusive," I said and eased down onto my bed.

"*Callicore aurelia.* What do you think?" She held the book up and pointed to a small butterfly with red on the tops of its wings and the numbers 89 outlined in black on the undersides.

"Numbers on its wings?"

"The butterfly doesn't know it has numbers on its wings, Gwen. Humans concocted that meaning. It's a design pattern that's supposed to deter predators. It'll be hard to get. I've never seen so much as an egg for sale in my catalog."

"That's you to a tee," I closed my eyes, "only the rare and the beautiful."

"You say that like it's a bad thing."

"You know something, Lila?"

"If you're going to insult me, save it."

I opened my eyes and watched her jot down notes on a little pad of paper.

"You never think you're going to miss your mom as much as you do."

She stopped writing. "Today is Sunday, Gwen. Can we save this topic for another day?"

"God, Lila, can you say something nice about her?"

"You think your mother dies and you're not going to suffer?"

"I miss her, Lila."

"I watch you and I think how I should call my own mom. But I don't. Do you see me calling her? You wear her present more than I do. She doesn't even know I have hair. Mrs. Parker's been taking me to the hospital for months, not her. I don't know if I'm going to audition next month or not, but when I do go to Portland, it'll be for professional reasons and not to live with my mother. And you know what? I'll survive. I plan on doing quite well without her."

"Of course you're going to audition next month," I said.

Lila closed her book and set it neatly on the stack by her bed. She stretched out on her back and lifted one thin, perfectly shapely leg, calf muscles more developed than any girl's at school. Her skirt fell down and I could see her underwear. She made swishing movements with her leg, keeping it straight while her toe flexed and then pointed.

"My teacher thinks I ought to take a summer workshop with the company and audition next year. I'll be eighteen by then, though. Time's passing."

She lowered her leg and rolled over to face me, propping her head up on her hand. "Dave Calhoun comes around my locker now. He stopped by a couple of times last week. He placed second in the state last fall. Did you know that?"

"Why don't our conversations ever go in a straight line, Lila?"

"I'm an athlete, he's an athlete. I have respect for that."

"You're going to go out with him?"

"I have to take what I can get, don't I?"

Thirty-seven

April arrived before Miz Hundy let me touch her hair. Cabbage White butterflies fluttered around town now like scraps of homework paper. Lila said they were on the wing early this year. Small white butterflies were thick on the path when I trailed kids down to the main building after math. Butterflies moved erratically through the woods where I continued to eat lunch alone, as if they'd overdone it on nectar, although these shifty survivors nectared on blackberry and dogwood, according to Lila, and—once people got their act together—vegetable gardens. White wings fluttered in the long grass behind Mrs. Parker's house and singly and in pairs on the cement walk out front. No doubt about it, spring was here.

Miz Hundy said she could spare an hour on Wednesday in between working at the barn and Happy Hour. I bargained hard for Saturday. I told her the job required at least two hours. I won. Saturday morning Lila had to be climbing her ballet teacher's stairs at ten to ten. This gave me enough time to swing by Safeway and buy mint they had in little cartons out front and a small bag of potting soil. Our screen door had lost more paint this winter. I held it open and worked my key into our back doorknob. Our kitchen was bare and filled with silence. How many conversations had soaked into the walls over the years? Arguments and shouting these last few years, but also "Pass the ketchup, honey?" and "How'd it go at the barn today?" All those conversations couldn't be gone. If I only had the key I could unlock them from the walls.

Loneliness was a feeling I was used to and was nothing to stop me. Using my car key I ripped open the bag of soil and cupped my hands under the tap for a watering can. A big white butterfly landed on the planter box before I'd even tamped the soil around my mint—two black spots on each wing, a female.

Miz Hundy yelled hello from the sidewalk and I wiped my hands on my jeans and yelled, *be right there.* I already felt gloom lifting, just seeing her standing there in beige jodhpurs and riding jacket the reddish brown of several of her horses, her lively face upturned, cig in her tough old hand.

"Careful on those damned stairs," she said, watching me come down. "They're a lawsuit waiting to happen."

"You never did quit smoking, Miz Hundy. Weren't you going to quit?"

"Never say never, gal."

The day was mild and Mrs. Parker had the shop door propped open with a box of conditioner. She stood on a ladder near the front counter, holding a drill. No houses to clean today and the lady wore black stretch pants and a tiny pink sweater pushed up her massive arms. Her headband was a strip of white terry cloth, like tennis players used.

She already had several hooks in the ceiling. Strings of blue beads waited in boxes on the counter. She'd hung them aleady from ceiling to floor in the rear of the shop.

"Are you telling fortunes, sister?" Miz Hundy growled, shrugging out of her jacket and folding it neatly on the counter. She nodded at the black velvet curtain nailed over the front window.

Dishwater blond hair was strewn underneath my mom's red chair. The broom was in the back closet. "Mrs. Parker, you have to keep things tidy," I called. "Customers notice stuff like this."

"The Kohler twins were in." The lady shrugged, still perched on her ladder. "I haven't had a chance to clean up yet."

"You didn't take much off."

"Their mother ordered me not to."

"Mrs. Kohler didn't ask you for highlights? She never makes an appointment, but she always comes in with her daughters and expects you to drop everything and give her highlights."

"Probably goes to Portland now," Mrs. Parker said gloomily. Frowning, and with a determined look on her face, she pushed her drill into Miz Hundy's plank ceiling.

"Sit down, Miz Hundy!" I said, patting my mom's chair. My stomach was awkward but every bit of hair got swept into the dustpan.

The woman on the ladder took her finger off the trigger and blessed quiet returned to the shop. "You're going to apply a relaxer first, aren't you?" she said.

"You can do it if you want the practice."

"I'm busy adding style to this place, Gwen," Mrs. Parker pouted, her little mouth puckering in her heavy face. "You shouldn't be doing physical activity when you're pregnant. I was going to clean up."

"One reason my mother was so successful, Mrs. Parker?" I dumped hair into the wastebasket. "This place was immaculate, capital I, at all times."

"Are you going to compare me to her twenty-four hours a day?" Nona Parker said mournfully, drooping one arm over the top of her ladder. For such a heavy lady she seemed comfortable off the ground.

"*Up*, Miz Hundy." I patted the red seat. At the front window I took a handful of black velvet and yanked it off its nail.

"You have to let light in, Mrs. Parker, that's another rule of success."

"It took me an hour to hang that up! Leslie?" She gave her sister a pleading look.

"I didn't like it either, Nona." Miz Hundy settled into the red chair. "Leave things the way they were is my advice. Gwen? I'm going to rent upstairs to Fuentes."

"Oh, fuck that."

"Language, Gwen," the lady clucked.

I dropped a plastic poncho over her clean white blouse and got busy squirting relaxing solution onto her half grown-out perm, working the solution from her roots to her damaged ends.

"We'd get him out of his van and give him a roof over his head. You'd have child care at arm's length."

"He's pretty attached to his van."

"I'm going to put the idea to him."

"Come on, Miz Hundy, I don't want this stuff on long. I have to rinse you."

I had her back in the red chair and my mom's pink hair dryer going full blast when Lila walked through the open door. Her leotard was visible under her denim jacket. She wore loose jeans and new black boots with silver buckles she'd bought over the phone from Portland.

I clicked off the hair dryer. "You're done with lessons already? What are you doing here, Lila?"

"I'm a paying customer!" She swung her leg out to the side and did a neat little pirouette. "I want you to do something to my hair."

I glanced at Nona Parker in the terry-cloth headband still standing on the ladder. "You could wash it and put some gel in it. Give her a spiky look."

"Couldn't you? I want to get all these hooks in."

"I'm busy, and walk-ins are always welcome." I gave Lila a long look. "When you're a walk-in, you can't always expect immediate attention, though."

Miz Hundy gave her sister a sympathetic smile. "You're stuck with her, Nona."

"What have you done to me, gal!" was Miz Hundy's response thirty minutes later. She fingered her wet hair, the color of river mud, and grimaced at her reflection.

"Have a little faith, Miz Hundy, I'm not finished."

I worked the scissors fast through her hair, leaving clean edges. "Could I come out to the barn sometime? Just to clean tack or something?"

"You're cutting it awfully short, aren't you?"

"It'll be even shorter when it's dry. Nobody can clean tack like I can, Miz Hundy."

"Those girls will have you grooming their mounts and doing all their work for them before you know it. My barn isn't the place for a girl who's going to deliver a baby in a month."

"You can chain me to a sawhorse, Miz Hundy. I promise I'll stay in the tack room."

"Speaking of my barn." Miz Hundy touched her hair. She wore a slightly more hopeful expression now that I'd cut off the damage, giving a clean line to her jaw. "I sold your doctor friend my camper. He wanted dash AC. I told him since I was practically giving it away, what did he expect? Just take the cardboard off the broken window."

"The window's broken?"

"Vandals," she sighed.

"I thought you used your camper for a waiting room, Miz Hundy?"

"Mothers today," the woman shook her head, "they're all too busy to even get out of their cars. They toot their horn and if their daughters don't come running, boy do I hear about it."

I ran the comb through her clean, healthy-looking hair. "Do you know when in June he leaves?"

"Mid-May, actually. They agreed to let him out of his contract a month early if he'll return to the hospital this September."

"Mid-May! That's when I'm due!"

"He wants to beat the college kids to Wyoming."

"I thought he was climbing in the Cascades?"

"He's got months, gal, for every hair-brained scheme he can possibly cook up."

"He's coming back in fall, Miz Hundy. Is that what you said? We can have him over for dinner at your apartment again."

"Get me dried and let's see what you've done to me, gal."

My mom's hair dryer and the styling brush had the woman looking ten years younger in no time. The color defined the frank steeliness in her eyes and softened her

mouth. A Hank Williams song came out of my mouth
while I worked. My mom played it practically every day.

> *A jug of wine to ease my mind,*
> *But what good does it do*
> *The jug runs dry but still I cry,*
> *I can't escape from you*

Thirty-eight

Hank Williams was on the stereo that night last August when my mom came home and swung her red purse at my head. I was lying on the couch reading a magazine, waiting up for her. I had no time to duck.

"It's all over town! He's old enough to be your father!"

I rubbed my chin and the side of my face where she'd clocked me. "Come on, Mom, it's no big deal."

She cradled a bottle of wine in her arms and marched into her bedroom. I gave her time to make a dent in it, knocked and entered.

"Gwen, I don't want to talk to you right now." She was lying on her clean white bedspread, one arm thrown over her eyes.

I crossed her room and sat down on the long white bench under her slide-up windows and waited. Her windows were cracked and a cool breeze stirred the hot air in her room. The chainsaw shop across our alley was dark, but they always kept a light on in the window above the big McCullough, the blade long enough to cut old growth, not that we had any left in our woods. Loggers always stopped, though, to admire the saw, and then continued on to the tavern down the street.

"All I can say is you damn well better have used protection, oh daughter of mine. If you end up pregnant—well, I just won't stand for it."

She pulled her arm off her eyes and sat up. "I'm going to ask this once. Did he hurt you?"

"Edgar?" I snickered. "All that dope he smokes, Mom? He couldn't hurt a fly."

"Could he get it up?"

"Oh . . . yeah."

She looked disappointed. "How long has it been going on between you two?"

"Do you want the truth?"

"Jesus. That long?"

She scrabbled around on the nightstand for her wine. "I'm sorry you never knew your grandmother, Gwen. Every day I wake up and ask God to give me one good reason not to follow her."

"Your business is a reason, Mom."

"But you're not? You're not a reason?"

I lifted my glasses and peered at my mother. A square chin, mole on her left cheek, thick blonde hair without a trace of gray, parted cleanly in the middle. She sat like a man, legs apart, elbows on her knees.

"Don't look at me like that," she said, irritated. "He lives on wheels, honey. He's been here two years already, two years too long, probably. He'll want to take you with him."

She answered her own question: "I've raised you with one eye on what I was doing. What do I expect? Of course you're going to leave me."

My mother's steps were heavy as she crossed her bedroom floor. The bathroom door closed, she turned on the shower. I knew she was crying.

Thirty-nine

The following Friday afternoon Lila dropped into my passenger seat and hissed, "He asked me out! Dave Calhoun asked me out!" Whizzing out of the parking lot because I preferred to leave school as quickly as possible.

"He's asked you out about fifteen times, Lila," I replied, "you keep saying no. Put on your belt."

"This time I said yes! We're going running together tomorrow afternoon. We're only going a few blocks, I don't need my belt."

"That's your date? Running?"

"We're starting slow," Lila shrugged.

"I didn't know you could run." We were at the opposite end of Fifteenth now, the intersection with Addison.

"When you get your body back you can come with us."

"Just what Dave wants, I'm sure." I turned down Addison

and pulled to the curb in front of a ramshackle gray house with her teacher's ballet studio on the second floor.

Lila gathered up her backpack and her tote bag and paused with one leg out the door. "Dave asked me to sit with him at lunch today. I sat at Connie's table. Dennis was there? He didn't look at me. He sat right across the table and ignored me. He had his arm around his girlfriend—"

"What's her name." I nodded.

"He didn't bring up the hatchery. You ought to come in from the woods. You don't know what you're missing."

"I like my own company, Lila."

The girl bounded up the stairs and into the old building. A few minutes later her face and arms appeared at the window above me, as she warmed up at the barre.

Forty

I continued to sing at the tavern that night and every Friday night. I hardly got nervous anymore. I sat in my chair on the stage with my belly resting between my thighs and sang six, seven, sometimes ten songs. I sang until I got the finger across the throat from Miz Hundy. At the bar afterward I'd drink my Sprite and ladies would come up and ask me when I was due—any day now, by the look of me—and did my legs and back ache and what foods did I crave?

By the third week in April I couldn't wait any longer. My body craved horses. That Saturday broke cloudy but warm, and I drove up the highway with the window down and Linda Rondstadt on the tape deck. My audience kept requesting her songs.

I parked in my usual spot under the hemlock tree and circled the barn. The camper was still parked on the north side, cardboard from a U-Haul box jammed into its broken passenger window.

Miz Hundy was in the ring shouting at Connie, who sat on Gallant with her knees drawn up under her like a jockey. "Use kinder hands, gal."

Noon came and went. I had a thermos of weak coffee and a sandwich in my truck. All of a sudden Connie stood in the tack room doorway with an expensive bridle over her shoulder.

"Do you like it?" she said, arranging it in front of me on my makeshift work table. The snaffle bit was coated with Gallant's saliva. "It's a birthday present from my folks."

I couldn't help running my finger across the rich brown leather of the headstall.

"You're the only one in town who gets eight-hundred-dollar birthday presents, Connie."

"Oh, it didn't cost that much."

"With all that silver inlay? You want to bet?"

"My birthday party's a week from today, Gwen. Are you going to come?"

I turned my light dressage saddle upside down on the planks that spanned two wobbly sawhorses and rubbed hard with my soapy cloth.

"Why do you want a pregnant girl at your party?"

"One of these days you're going to understand you fascinate me, Gwen."

"Are you inviting Lila?"

"I'm inviting Dave Calhoun. He'll invite her."

I wrung my sponge out in my bucket and shoved my hair out of my face. "I'll bet you're overjoyed to have her back in your crowd, Connie, and there's nothing you can do about it."

A cagey look came over the girl's face. "Dennis Bly promised to come. He's caused trouble between you two. I don't want any cat-fighting at my party."

"Lila and I settled that. We are so over that." I continued to move my sponge in small circles, cleaning in the crevices of the saddle where stirrups buckled on.

Connie laughed under her breath. "As badly as he's treated you, Gwen, you still have a thing for him."

"I'm cleaning a saddle, Connie, I'd like to do it in peace. Please get your bridle out of my way."

She pulled off her helmet and fluffed her creamy blonde hair. She went down to Portland to have it highlighted and cut every six weeks. I could do as good a job.

"Dennis isn't serious about Margaret Livesy, Gwen."

"Then he's not a very nice person, is he?" I said.

"In some ways he's not, no."

I glanced at her. "Well, you're honest, for once."

"It's because I have a weak brother. I'm accustomed to coddling boys. It's all I know how to do."

"I didn't dare look to see if Agnes is gone," I murmured.

"She's gone," Connie said.

"You trailered her to Dr. Kazlowski's daughter in Michigan?"

"We sold her to a stable across the river. They're going to use her for total, total beginning hunt seat. She'll be OK. Getting back to Dennis?" Connie pulled off her gloves finger by finger. "What kind of girl would an insecure boy like him choose? A girl who worships the ground he walks on. Margaret and Lila are a lot the same that way, except my friend's not dying."

"Lila's in remission, Connie. If you say something like that again I'll smack your ass."

"You talk tough, but you'd do a lot to have Dennis."

I began buckling the stirrups back onto the saddle.

"You bluff girls, you'd never settle for a life at the salmon hatchery."

"Would you, Gwen?"

"He's not polished like your brother, Arthur. He's not talented at anything except clubbing salmon in the brain, and actually Lila surpassed him in that skill. He's a good runner, but where did that ever get anyone?"

I stood up and swung the saddle over my shoulder. "I always meant to get a tape of your brother's violin playing. I don't like Arthur much, but I loved how he played. That was the one good thing about staying in your house that summer."

"You mean for all of two days?" she sniffed, curling her hair behind her ear. "You should have stayed longer, Gwen. Your life wouldn't have taken this . . . turn."

I nodded. "I'm free, though. If this is how my life is going to go, oh well. I'll ride it where it takes me. It's my life. And I actually have two pretty decent ladies looking out for me. I have more than you think, Connie."

She stepped aside and I brushed past her and up the breezeway and entered fat old Red's stall. The mare nickered and bumped my belly with her head, waking up my daughter. *This is Red, my favorite. She's twenty-five, worn out and old, but she can still get out there in the arena and perform a nice dressage move. Don't be fooled. Take a whiff of this place. Smells pretty good, doesn't it? It's about all I have to pass on to you that's worth anything.*

I hung the clean piece of tack over the half stall door, a nice little surprise for Miz Hundy's one o'clock. I smelled Connie's perfume as she passed. "Don't forget my party, Gwen."

Forty-one

Dave Calhoun picked Lila up early the following Friday. They were going for burgers before Connie's party. If you placed second in the state in cross-country, you didn't need to dress up for Connie Beller. Dave wore what he always wore: jeans, flannel shirt, ball cap and thick running shoes. Lila wore makeup, nice black pants and a green shirt, unbuttoned enough from the bottom to show her tiny waist and bellybutton. She'd put gel in her hair and dried it spiky. Dave wouldn't be the only guy with his eye on her tonight.

"You have her home by eleven," Mrs. Parker said, and Dave looked surprised. "The party doesn't even begin til nine."

"Eleven-thirty, and that's my final offer," Mrs. Parker said.

I took a shower and piddled around getting ready. I was crazy to go, as pregnant as I was. All the girls would ignore me, guys would stare at me as if they'd never seen a belly my size before. How did they think they'd come into the world? Some football player would bump me and then say, oh, sorry! Some other guy would pinch me. They'd all laugh, ha ha ha. But here I was, putting on basically what Calhoun wore, jeans and a flannel shirt and work boots. I applied lipstick and brown eye shadow I found in the bathroom drawer and I parted my hair on the side and held it with a pink barrette. I mentally dressed my daughter at the same time. She was coming too, wasn't she? I imagined her curled up in my belly, sucking her thumb. I was born bald, so scratch a hair ribbon. I mentally sorted through the baby clothes Mrs. Parker had been buying me for weeks now and picked out a blue terry cloth sleeper and sky blue blanket.

Mrs. Parker knocked on the bedroom door and came in. "Are you really up for this, honey?"

Staring into space, I roused myself with an effort. "I'm not due for two weeks and five days, Mrs. Parker. I told you, if I feel contractions I'll let you know."

"I'm just afraid you won't know what they are."

"Like a big hand grabbing my belly down between my legs, my doctor said."

"You won't have any beer tonight?"

"I hate the taste of beer."

"You'll keep an eye on Lila?"

"I think Calhoun will be doing that, Mrs. Parker."

She settled onto Lila's bed and laid her heavy forearms in her lap. The ends of her dark red hair fell forward, still curled tight from the iron this morning.

"Do you think you have enough baby clothes? I could stop by the discount store Monday. You need more burp rags and more undershirts. I wish I could have found time to knit you a cap and sweater."

"Mrs. Parker, you have two jobs."

"Two jobs," she sighed. "That's a laugh." Freckles covered the backs of her tiny, fat hands.

"Business will pick up at the shop."

"I'd like to call it a salon."

"Mrs. Parker, do we have to change that many things?"

"Gwen, please, I need to have a few ideas."

"All right. It's a salon."

"I'll be so relieved when you deliver, honey. I'm on pins and needles waiting. I'm on edge."

"It blows me away, Mrs. Parker." I rested my arm over my stomach. "This will be a baby in a couple of weeks. I'm going to be her mother. I'm going to be responsible for her."

"I know, honey. Go on, and try to forget it for tonight." She stood up, smoothing out her black stretch pants, the same kind Lila left the house wearing. "You won't be able to change a diaper without bumping into my sister or me, if that's any comfort."

Forty-two

The Bellers lived on the bluff east of the high school, so they and their neighbors quite literally looked down on the rest of town. Their brick house with white pillars had so many cars parked in the driveway and down the street, I had to drive all the way to the end, to the cul-de-sac full of beauty bark, and walk back. Dave Calhoun's silver Mustang was parallel parked politely between a yellow Ford and a small pickup, but the wheel of Dennis's Toyota was on the neighbor's lawn. He'd come early to get a parking place like that. I tried not to think about him. At the same time, I tried to fix the smile on my face I would wear when I did see him. As if to say, you're no big deal. It wasn't hard to ignore him at school. Geometry was our only class where we sat near each other. I generally arrived just before the bell rang and he was the first one out the door when class was over. At a party it would be different. We'd have no desk between us and no math test, just our hands and maybe a drink, although nothing alcoholic for me.

Mr. Beller himself answered the front door. I had quit trying to button my coat days ago and he openly stared at me. The one time Lila would have come in handy. The man's disapproval was hard to face alone.

Finally he said, "You're friends with my daughter?"

My hand in my pocket hefted the silver locket wrapped in pink tissue. "No, but she invited me anyway."

He was a small man with a shiny bald head. The great-grandson-or-something of the man who built the first sawmill down on the river, long ago, when fur trappers still roamed the area, and the Cathlemets camped on the river, droves of them.

Mr. Beller stepped back into his beautiful house and said, "Come in. Hurry, now. The heat's escaping."

He shook his newspaper in the direction of the kids across the room, grouped on the bottom of the staircase. Then he stepped down into his sunken living room and his large TV.

Not much had changed in two, nearly three, years. The same art work was on the walls, same earth-tone pillows and throws on the white leather couch. If you pressed your face to the big windows you could see the winking lights of Kelso across the Cowlitz River. No sign of Mrs. Beller. Saturday nights might be big nights to shop.

The kids on the stairs wouldn't move and I shoved hard to get through them. Our entire junior class was packed into the rec room, it seemed, and more kids lounged outside the bathroom.

The pool table was heavy with coolers and I felt better

with a can of 7-Up in my hand. I made a big deal out of opening it, as if it required a lot of concentration, because some of the kids were openly staring. I gulped fizz and got busy lighting a cigarette. Here I was, pregnant and smoking, the looks they gave me!

"Hey, they're ultra lights," I wanted to shout, "I'm hardly inhaling!" Was I that weird? Did I deserve this?

Where was Lila? Here was Connie's brother, though, the violinist. Arthur ambled over and took my arm and led me to the window that overlooked the crowded driveway.

"Hello." He hadn't shaved in a few days, but maybe that was on purpose, and I noticed two other things: his blue eye didn't take a single glance at my stomach and the kids had gone back to flirting and swallowing beer.

"You're someone interesting to talk to, Gwen."

I tapped my cig into my can of pop. "If this house is no-smoking, boy, do I have egg on my face."

"Connie's little friends are so boring. God, give me whatever you're smoking."

"The smell will get into your clothes, Arthur." Handed him my pack.

"You're smoking air," he said, disappointed.

"Arthur, is being pregnant that bad for a person's social life? Is it the worst that could happen?"

He drew smoke into his lean body and exhaled toward a knot of senior guys jabbing each other in the ribs in the corner. "That's why I'm talking to you, wanted to help you out a little."

I laughed. "Well, you're honest."

"You have to be when your sister impersonates your mother, and does enough calling to get you invited back to your conservatory. I get the pleasure of driving all the way back to Philadelphia for another audition. I'm a bad influence on my sister. She thinks all guys are as high-maintenance as me."

"Right now Connie's focused on a high-maintenance horse by the name of Gallant. I don't think she has time for boys," I said.

"That's what she says, anyway."

"She's out at the barn all the time—"

"Damn it, Pérez, you keep bumping into me." I turned to see Coover from math class standing right behind me.

"*I* bump into *you?*" I snorted. "You don't own the room."

Arthur clucked and shook his head. He took my arm and pulled me deeper into the crowded room, but not before I saw a pair of gold eyes near the door. Dennis looked away quickly, his dark-haired girlfriend beside him.

Arthur brought me right up to Connie, sitting on a couch under the eaves. "Why don't you invite her to take a load off, Con."

"You came, Gwen." Connie sounded surprised. She wore a pleated skirt and a tight American flag T-shirt that showed off her perfect seventeen-year-old breasts. She didn't get up.

"Doesn't everybody, when you call, Connie?" I looked around for an ashtray. Should I give her her present now?

In his crisp linen pants and pale blue shirt Arthur drifted off. He was at least two years older than anyone else in the room.

As if she could read my mind, Connie shrugged. "My parents said I have to have a chaperone. He's better than my dad."

"Sounds like he's heading back to music school," I said. Connie nodded. "If he can only keep his mouth shut."

"Connie! Happy birthday!" Margaret Livesy came up and threw her arms around her friend's neck.

Connie rolled her eyes, "Margaret, you're strangling me."

"Where are you putting your presents?" The girl's slim arms were bare. Around her left wrist, one silver bangle. Her package was also wrapped in silver, with tiny pink balloons, about the size of a book.

"In my bedroom," Connie replied.

"Here." I pulled the gift box from my coat and handed it to Margaret. "Put that with the rest of them, will you?"

"You brought me a present, Gwen?"

"That's what people do at birthday parties. Happy birthday, by the way."

"You could take her coat too, Margaret. Gwen, everyone's coats go in my room."

"I'll keep mine, thanks."

Connie arched an eyebrow. "Not going to stay long?"

"Margaret?" I said to the waiting girl. "What are you waiting for? Hop to it, and make sure my present goes on top of the stack."

"Is it fragile?" Margaret frowned. Shy and small-boned. Go figure what Dennis saw in her.

"What difference does it make? Put it on top."

"Do what she says, Margaret."

The girl turned obediently and threaded her way toward the rec room door, bangle slid up to her elbow, presents in her arms.

"Will you look at them?" Connie groaned. Bodies had shifted and we could clearly see in the center of the room Dennis and Dave Calhoun and a few other guys lugging ice chests off the pool table.

"I should have hidden the balls," Connie murmured.

"The birthday girl wants them to socialize." She didn't move to stop them, though. She continued to sit while I stood. An ache had started low in my back and was only getting worse.

"Can I have one?" Connie nodded at the ultra light I was stubbing out on my pop can.

"Have the pack. I shouldn't be smoking."

"I just want one."

She leaned over and used the beige rug for an ashtray. I couldn't quite bring myself to do the same. I got another one going and used my full can of pop as an ashtray and tried to recall which day Mrs. Parker came up here to clean.

"Is everybody going out to the river later?" Lila materialized at my elbow, gulping beer. "Everyone still does that, right, Connie? They go to the river?"

"It's a little cold still, Lila. Excuse me, please. This is my party and I've got to mingle. Dennis is using the cue my father doesn't let anyone, not even Arthur, touch. Thank you for the present, Gwen, I'll open it later." Connie slipped through bodies, toward the pool table.

Pretty girls in the senior class moved in and filled her couch under the eaves. I didn't have a chance. They sat shoulder to shoulder in their little skirts, faces hostile, legs long and bare. The couch arm was available, though that one's skinny arm would have to move or get crushed by my butt.

Then Dennis arrived from thin air, a pool cue in his gloved hand. The expensive one that only Connie's father was allowed to touch? That would be Dennis's luck.

"You need a chair, Pérez?"

Here it was, the big moment. We were talking. I couldn't think of anything to say, so I put my cigarette in my mouth.

"You were the early bird tonight to get your parking place, Dennis."

"Look. You shouldn't be standing, as pregnant as you are." He took my arm and tried to pull me over to the couch. I shrugged him off.

"Leave me alone."

"I wish we were alone," he muttered. "I want to talk to you."

He blew his bangs out of his eyes. His black gloves lent him a dangerous, mysterious air. Had he grown since I'd seen him last? "I really just want to find somewhere quiet and talk to you, Pérez."

"Dennis, I am so over you."

"Hey!" Bodies parted and Lila was beside me again, gulping her beer. "Are you going to keep Dave busy all night playing pool or do I get some of his attention?"

"Lila," Dennis said, taking a fresh grip on his pool cue, "this is a party, people mingle. You don't stay joined at the hip at parties." He swallowed his own beer and looked around for a place to put his can.

"Take Dennis for example," I said. "Is he with Margaret, the love of his life? No."

Lila's cool blue eyes looked the boy over. A look I had received many times. "Why aren't you with your girlfriend, Dennis?"

"You dames. Jesus."

He let go of my arm and turned to Lila, lowering his head to talk directly into her face. "Remember those Coho you helped spawn last fall? The babies are in pens now."

"Coho, my ass." Lila swigged beer and wiped the back of her hand across her mouth, smearing her lipstick. "Let's get some beer and go out to the river."

"She really wants to get Dave away from the pool table," I snickered.

"Sounds good to me," Dennis said. "I'll tell Connie."

"I'm going home," I said, "if Connie comes."

Dennis thumbed the brim of his cap lower, over his eyes. Under his flannel shirt he wore a clean white T-shirt that made his neck look even more tanned. "It's Connie's birthday, Pérez, I don't think she'd appreciate it if we all took off without her."

"Did you guys hear anything I said?" Lila demanded. "Dave is *my* date tonight, Dennis."

The guy leaned so close to me his lips brushed up against my ear. "I'd like to explain a few things about Margaret and me."

"You'd better slow down on the beer, Dennis, you're forgetting you brought her to this party."

His breath lifted gooseflesh on the back of my neck. "I have to go out with someone, don't I, Pérez, while I wait around for you?"

Someone turned the music up louder. I could hardly hear what he said next.

"Kind of wish I'd played my cards different with you, is what I'm saying."

"Fine!" Lila shouted. "Forget it, both of you!" She stormed over to the pool table, knocking into people as she went, and thumped Dave Calhoun on the arm. The music was on pretty loud, I couldn't hear what she said to him, but he calmly took her beer from her hand and laid it on the felt, shrugged, and handed her his cue. Be my guest, said his hand gesture. She bent over to line up a shot. She had strong, slender lines to her body. Calhoun had no idea how she could swing a baseball bat. He had no idea of the tough center underneath Lila's delicate surface.

"I'm going to find you a chair," Dennis shouted. "And then we're going to talk. People do that at parties. They talk."

As much beer as he'd had, he slipped through the crowded room with long-legged grace, the tail of his shirt hanging loose over his butt. He had a way of threading through bodies without bumping into anyone, nobody slowed him down.

The wall of the rec room was right behind me. I wanted to slide down and sit on the floor, but the problem would be getting up again. Behind my shut eyes I found peace and quiet in spite of the pounding music. And then Lila was plucking at my coat sleeve. My heavy suede coat made me stand out, I knew that. The other girls wore light sweaters. Some, like Margaret Livesy, had bare arms.

"Dennis is in the hall talking to Connie."

"I thought you were playing pool, Lila?"

"I saw Dennis leave, I followed him. Gwen, she caught him. All night she's been waiting for her chance. They're laughing." Lila's eyes glowed.

"Shouldn't you be telling this to his girlfriend?" I said.

So many bodies between me and the rec room door and water pooling in the corners of my eyes, on the lenses of my glasses. All my own fault, of course. All my own fault.

Made it to the front door and heaven walking through it and closing it on the noise and stupid problems of high school. Too early yet for kids to have spilled outside. The empty driveway was lit by lamps buried near the brick wall that divided the Bellers from the house one over. I struck a match for the last cigarette of my pack and maybe ever, in my life. In the flower beds rhododendrons and dogwoods calmly passed the night. A bench sat under a rose trellis, no blooms yet.

The front door opened, spilling light and noise. Dennis hollered, "You walked right by me, Gwen."

"You were busy." I didn't turn around. The night was mild, my heavy coat completely unnecessary.

"I can't wish Connie happy birthday? What's wrong with you?"

"You wanted to be alone with me," I murmured. "Well? We're alone."

He strode down the driveway and stopped a few feet from me. "Who do you think you are?"

I dropped my half-smoked cigarette under my boot and kicked it off the driveway. "Good night, Dennis."

He grabbed my arm. "She doesn't own me."

"She can live at the hatchery with you, Dennis, one of them, Margaret or Connie. Take your hand off me."

"You're not listening to me."

"I'm too pregnant. You can hardly look at me."

"I'm afraid to look at you, Pérez."

"We're having our first conversation for the month of April and the month is almost over, Dennis." I was tired, I tried to pull free.

"Don't you pull away, Pérez, until I've finished saying what I've got to say. You want to talk about the hatchery? We'll talk about it. They're making me assistant manager after I graduate. Just heard today. I'll get my own house, paid for. None of those females upstairs would touch a house so far out of town. Kind of wonder if you'd be interested. There it is."

"Dennis!" Connie stood in her open front door. "They're fighting! You have to come!"

"In a minute." He didn't let go of me.

"Coover said something . . . rude to Lila! Dave hit him. You'd better come."

"Calhoun can take care of himself."

"Dennis! It's my birthday. What if something gets broken?"

Dennis turned to stare up the driveway at the girl backlit in the front door. "Can't your brother do something?"

"Arthur can't injure his bow hand!"

"Christ Almighty." Dennis turned back to me and whispered, "Pérez, I know you're going to leave, but I'm asking you not to. I'm asking you to wait." He covered the drive in long steps. Connie grabbed him and pulled him over the threshhold. At the same time Lila flew past them, out the open door, saving me the effort of going in to find her.

"I want to go home," she snapped.

I nodded. "I'm really tired of repeating myself, but that's where I'm going."

Forty-three

We were in the bathroom, wiping off makeup. I asked Lila to fill me in. "Dave stood up for your honor, huh?" I tried to make a joke out of it, but her face wouldn't switch gears from seriousness to light.

"Coover's a jerk," she said.

Actually, she was the only one wiping off makeup. I was sitting on the bathtub, watching her.

She unbuttoned her blouse and dropped it into the clothes hamper and unhooked her bra. The scar above her breast was smaller than the one on Dennis's hand and not yet pale. That would require time. She noticed me watching and turned away, shoving her arms into her pajama top.

"I hope you were telling Dennis to fuck off on the driveway. I hope you were, but something tells me you weren't,

Gwen." She gave serious attention to each tiny pearl button in her pajama top.

"That's kind of a hard-line approach, Lila."

"Did your mother make you this way? Willing to settle for so little?"

"So? What do you think of Dave?"

"I couldn't get him alone to form an opinion and you know it."

"It's tough to compete with a pool table, Lila. What did Coover say that was so insulting?"

"It involved you, Gwen, as if you don't know."

"So Calhoun was standing up for me?"

"No, he was defending me. Dave doesn't like you." She stalked into the bedroom.

I closed the bathroom door and started shedding clothes. The hot water felt incredible and when my entire body was soaped, I hung onto the soap holder and cleaned in between my toes and ran my hand in between my legs and let water hit my baby hard. My hair streamed water. Water filled my mouth and hit the back of my throat. The ache was still there in my lower back. According to the baby books Mrs. Parker had given me, you couldn't get rid of it. You had to be patient.

Forty-four

Monday I stopped by our old apartment to see with my own two eyes Edgar Fuentes painting. I found him in our living room, standing on a folding chair. From behind he looked thinner, his long hair held back in a rubber band. He dabbed ivory paint onto the dark crown molding and must have heard me come up the back stairs, but didn't turn around.

"Miz Hundy's making you do the hard part."

Finally he gave me a glance. "You shouldn't breathe these fumes, kid."

"I shouldn't smoke either. Ultra lights, but still." I waved my Pall Mall at him.

"The lady said no smoking on her property."

"Dope, Edgar, not cigarettes. So? Are you abiding by that rule?"

"One day at a time, kid."

He wore a white T-shirt and baggy jeans. His feet on the chair were bare.

"Because if you ever get any dope in my daughter's lungs," I rubbed my belly, "you are so over, Edgar."

"Your mother was protective of you in the beginning." He nodded. "I seem to remember that. She wouldn't let you off the deck. You probably don't remember much about that side of her? She wouldn't let you ride your tricycle in the road. Thought some logger would come along, driving too fast. She lost it, though. That was my impression when I returned. She no longer seemed to notice you much at all."

"We're not going to talk about my mother."

"All right." He set his brush across his paint can and got off the chair. "What do you want to talk about?"

"I just wanted to see you."

He came toward me and pulled me into his arms. He smelled like paint, a pleasant smell.

"OK, you can let go now," I said.

He dropped his arms obediently. "Can I?" and he scooped his hand under my flannel shirt and rubbed my belly. With my eyes closed the sensation was soothing. His hand was warm and the little creature moved under his gentle pressure.

I grabbed his wrist. "That's enough, Edgar."

"You take after her."

"My mother?"

"The Hundy woman."

"Miz Hundy?"

"Bossy," he said mournfully.

From the kitchen I called, "What color do you want to do in here?" and when he came to stand beside me, I pointed at the sickly green walls. "We always meant to paint them. Somehow we never found the time."

"Yellow, I thought?"

"Pale, not too bright."

"There's plenty of room for you here." He leaned against the counter and looked at me. That quality of hesitation was back in his face.

"Why don't you find someone your own age, Edgar?" I said kindly, "I don't mean that in a bad way."

"You've got so many people to rely on now." He padded back into the living room and climbed back up on the folding chair. "My mother's still alive," he added. "You're so sure it's a girl. We could name her Mercedes."

"I was thinking Althea."

He turned to look at me, his long face grave. "Why do you want to put all that bad energy into our kid's life?"

"Thea for short."

After a minute he said, "Her last name will be Fuentes?"

"Are you going to deserve that honor?"

He turned back to the molding, dabbing at it with his tiny brush. "I fixed the knobs on the kitchen cabinets. I'd like to scrape the window sashes in here and repaint them. There's a lot I can do for the lady."

He was humming now as he worked.

Forty-five

The very next day, Tuesday, I began to feel the strange pulling down in my body that my doctor had warned me about. The feeling didn't really become strong enough to get my attention until math, and then I actually felt something powerful move through me. This kid I'd been growing all these months had a mind of her own—two weeks early on the nose. She had control of my body now. My heart pounded. Kids sat around me staring dumbly at their math books. The long months of waiting were over.

I walked out of class with everyone else, as if this was another day at the beach, and down the path to the main building. Dennis held the door open for me and then strode off down the hall. He hadn't spoken to me since the party. Unfinished business was like an electrical charge between us, but that wasn't my problem now. I

turned all my attention toward moving through the crowded hall.

Dave Calhoun was standing at Lila's locker.

"Come on," I took her arm.

"Let go of me!"

I have strong hands and I didn't let go. I pulled her
down the hall. Dave ran after us and so I stopped and said,
"Could I have a second of privacy with your girlfriend?"

He narrowed his gray eyes. "No, I don't think so."

Thank goodness for the girls' bathroom. I took a fresh
hold on Lila's bony wrist and banged through the door.
The bathroom was crowded. The whole damn school was
crowded. "I'm having it," I said into Lila's face.

Margaret Livesy was freshening up her makeup at the
mirror, running her powder puff under her dark bangs and
over her nose. She gave me a cool stare. I felt like saying,
"Oh please," but already I was conserving every bit of my
energy for what was to come.

"It?" Lila breathed.

"Can you drive a stick, Lila?"

"You know I can't."

"Well, come with me, will you?"

"Dave's waiting . . . "

"If he's going to be your boyfriend he'd better get used
to it. We have to go out the side door, if we get caught leaving school . . . " My voice trailed off. "I don't want to make
a big production out of this, OK? Keep your voice down
and act casual. They'll call Dr. Coleman from the hospital."

"Remind me to give you something from my collection,"
Lila babbled as we left the bathroom arm in arm, "when all
this is said and done."

The hall was less crowded now. Most of the kids were

in the cafeteria. Dave Calhoun lounged near the water fountain, but he jumped right over as soon as he saw us.

"Dave?" Lila said. "I'll meet you in there. Go on. Get our table and save me a seat."

"But—"

"*Dave*, would you just *do* as I *say?*"

We pushed out the side door into the last day of April. "I think I'd like to give you my Kite Swallowtail," Lila said, taking my arm and pulling me around the building.

"I can walk fine, Lila."

"Did your water break?"

"Am I wet? Even if I was, Dr. Coleman said that doesn't necessarily mean it's time to blast off, if you know what I mean. Oh, man." I stopped and leaned against the building.

"Gwen?" Lila's face was pinched and anxious.

"They're far apart, don't worry."

"Your bag's at home, your overnight bag?"

"Mrs. Parker can bring it." We were at my truck now. I never locked it. Lumbered up behind the wheel in no time.

"Because my Kite Swallowtail is my only specimen missing a tail and that's symbolic," Lila babbled as I backed up and swung out onto Fifteenth, driving away from Main toward Addison, the shortcut to the hospital.

"What with storms and cars, butterflies don't live very long, Gwen, and predators are a big, big problem, especially for the pretty ones. Better to lose a tail than get swallowed whole. All this time I've thought of Edgar Fuentes as the guy who snapped off your tail. I never told you, but I've always seen you as damaged but basically intact. I'm going to give you my imperfect specimen in honor of this baby."

Forty-six

My daughter was born in the early hours of May, a May baby. I named her Thea Leslie Nona Fuentes. "You didn't have to do that, gal," Miz Hundy, my first visitor, barked. "You didn't need to ingratiate yourself to us to keep us interested."

"It's done." I shrugged.

"Thea Leslie Nona *Fuentes?*"

I nodded.

"I approve. I approve," she said. She held a car seat in her arms, wrapped in pink ribbon, and she laid it at the foot of the bed. "Fuentes is painting my kitchen as we speak. We'll introduce him to Beautiful when we're ready. Where the hell is she?"

I pulled on jeans under my hospital gown. "Come on,"

and I led her out the door down the hall to the two-bed pediatric wing.

I kept my baby with me most of the rest of the day. I was the only new mom in the hospital and I had my room to myself. Little Thea was hungry constantly, and wouldn't stop screaming. The nurse told me to keep at it, keep trying to feed her. I didn't mind that she yelled. She had thick brown hair and light skin and hands that grasped at the air and my hair and fingers and anything that came her way. This was how she was going to make sense of the world, I could tell already—through her hands. I just held her and noticed everything, and when she fell asleep I used the time to jot down notes on the paper the nurse gave me. I tried to think of words to describe her, but all I came up with was stuff like warm, heavy, red, hungry. I wrote: *Her weight in my arms is everything,* and I dated that thought and signed my initials. When she woke up, I lifted her and tried to guide the little hole in her face to my nipple, and put her wrinkled red gums where they needed to be.

Mrs. Parker and Lila stopped in later in the day with slippers, a box of chocolates and a whole bag of baby clothes. Mrs. Parker had just come from work. She wore her brown skirt, white blouse and socks folded over her white sneakers.

"Your child has a poor suck reflex," she announced. "She needs a bottle. She's nothing but hungry."

"The nurse said I should keep trying to breastfeed her," I said.

"Where's this nurse? I may not have had a child of my own, Gwen, but I know babies. This one's hungry."

"Down the hall," I murmured. "There's a nurse down the hall."

After the woman stormed out on her little feet, Lila

rolled her eyes. "She's going to boss you from here to breakfast, so prepare yourself."

"Do you like the name Thea?" I replied.

"She doesn't exactly look like you, does she?"

"You want to hold her?"

Lila shrank away.

"Oh, come on." I patted the bed and Lila set her skinny butt down and took my baby's warm, surprisingly heavy body.

"Wow," she said. "Whooeee."

"Isn't she pretty, Lila? She's the prettiest thing."

"Here we are." Mrs. Parker breezed back into the room, a nurse behind her. "You see this little thing all head and mouth? Her cries are nothing more complicated than hunger. She's hungry! I want a bottle prepared for her on the double."

The nurse looked at my bodyguard, Nona Parker, feet rolling over the sides of her sneakers, heavy body buttoned and zipped into her work clothes. "I'll see what I can do."

Forty-seven

My baby arrived two weeks early, but in all other respects was perfectly healthy, so they wrote my name in a social worker's chart and Miz Hundy came to get me the following afternoon. We put my baby in the car seat and she slept the ten blocks home.

They were all waiting in the kitchen to welcome me home: Dr. Kazlowski, Lila, Mrs. Parker, Edgar Fuentes. The fern was on the counter, and a big cake and another car seat were in the center of the table. "That's from James," Miz Hundy said. "Great minds think alike. You can never have too many car seats."

They all *ooh*ed and *aah*ed over little Thea. Everyone wanted a chance to hold her.

Dr. Kazlowski held her like a professional, up against

his shoulder, bouncing her lightly. Thea pushed her little, perfect fingers into his hair and snuggled against him.

"I should have been an OB," he sighed. "Or a pediatrician, I'd have this all day."

"Kid favors you, Fuentes, as far as looks go, might as well be honest about it," Miz Hundy said, forking cake into her mouth. Her dark color had held and brunette defined everything that was tough and wonderful about her face.

"She has Gwen's nose," Nona Parker insisted. "And I think that's Althea reaching up from the grave in her chin. Am I the only one who sees it?"

"You're always seeing things, sister," Miz Hundy barked.

"Come on, that's Edgar's nose, Mrs. Parker," I said. "She's got *my* hands."

Edgar sat apart from the rest of us, behind the doctor, squeezed up against the wall. He sat quietly, although his eyes followed his daughter from pair of arms to arms. When Dr. Kazlowski passed the tiny girl back to Mrs. Parker so he could get up to refresh his punch, Edgar watched him and his face didn't relax until the doctor sat down again. When it was Edgar's turn he said no. "Oh, go on," everyone insisted, so he held what he was half responsible for making against his chest and she shrieked. Mrs. Parker said kindly, "Oh, she's hungry. I understand hunger. This one needs a bottle," and reached to take her back. Our tiny girl settled down immediately in her arms.

Lila took a very brief turn, but we all felt easier I think with little Thea in Nona Parker's arms. Then Dave Calhoun rang the doorbell.

Miz Hundy brought the guy into the kitchen and Lila said, "Dave!" All surprised.

"Didn't see you at school, Lila."

"Gwen's come home from the hospital. We're having a party."

"Dave, that's your name? Sit down," Miz Hundy boomed, "cut yourself some cake." She clapped him on the back.

Mrs. Parker waddled over to the counter where bottles were stacked a dozen deep. "Gwen, I'll let you breastfeed later. I'm sorry, but I've got to be firm. This little girl needs a bottle now or she'll cry all afternoon and I won't stand for it."

Miz Hundy pulled the car seat off the table. She said we'd put this one in my truck and keep the other one in her car. "You'll be driving her to the pediatrician and out to my barn. These things are perfectly safe. You're going to bring her out to my barn?"

"She's not putting that child in her pickup," Mrs. Parker said, pouring formula into a bottle. "I'll drive her if she has to go somewhere. And your barn is the last place this little girl is going."

Dave Calhoun continued to stand, shifting from one long foot to the other, and Lila stood beside him. Nobody had given him cake yet.

"Gwen went through labor, not you, Nona," Miz Hundy said calmly. "The child came out between her legs. She'll drive her and she'll use this car seat to do it." The tough old lady turned toward me. "You saw how I did it in my car? You use the seat belt. It's simple. The sooner you take her out in the world, the better. No coddling, now."

"Quit bossing Gwen around!" Mrs. Parker slammed the bottle into her microwave.

Lila caught my eye and raised her eyebrows as if to say, "This is your future, get used to it."

Forty-eight

I snuck my baby up to the cemetery the very next afternoon when Mrs. Parker was at work. I put my three-day-old daughter in her car seat and carried her out the front door, placing her carefully on the porch while I turned to lock the door. My belly had thinned out and my backaches and leg aches were gone. I felt light and easy in my body. However, I moved more slowly with Thea in my arms than I ever did when I was pregnant. I took her carefully down the front steps. So many little checks and stops and starts just to buckle the car seat in the front seat of my truck. She was awake, her dark eyes on my face. She loved to look at me and the feeling was mutual. I stood there on the sidewalk admiring her. I could have stared at her all day.

I had a bottle of formula in her baby bag and diapers and the rattle Lila gave me and the book *Where the Wild Things*

Are from Dr. Kazlowski, because it was never too soon to get your child started reading. The street was quiet. Even the doctor was at work, his last day. It was Friday, and right about now Lila would be walking the half-mile from school to her teacher's studio with her tote on her shoulder.

Mrs. Parker and Miz Hundy had put our bunk beds back together in our bedroom, leaving room under the window for Thea's crib. Lila had put up with it so far, but another arrangement would have to be made. I woke her up every time I got up to feed Thea.

As I was standing there thinking about all this stuff, a black Toyota swung around the corner. Dennis was behind the wheel. He drove slowly toward me and pulled into Mrs. Parker's spot in front of me. He got out and hesitated, pulled off his cap and whacked it against his thigh. "Ever coming back to school?" he said.

"I start summer school in June," I replied. Same gold eyes, high cheekbones, the carved salmon pretty, frozen mid-jump at his throat.

"Well, you might as well say hello to my baby, Dennis."

He stepped onto the sidewalk and peered in at her. She lay quietly in her car seat and returned his stare.

"Real pretty, Pérez, how come she doesn't have your nice blond hair?"

Dennis stepped back, gripping the chrome door handle with his gloved hand. "I just came by to say hi real quick, Pérez. That's all."

"So? You said it."

"Looks like I got you at a bad time."

"I'm going up to the cemetery to show her to my mom."

"Your mom, Pérez?"

"I only say things once now, Dennis. I don't repeat

myself. Shut that door, will you?" I circled my truck and opened the driver's door. "Nice talking to you, Dennis. See you around."

I pulled away from the curb and down to the guardrail to turn around. I kept glancing at my tiny girl but she looked OK, strapped in, as secure as I could make her. Her face was calm, tiny eyes open, ready to face me and the world squarely. I drove up the street slowly and braked at the stop sign. Took a deep breath, "Here we go, honey," and pulled out onto Main. Town fell away and then the river moved below us, as it is moving still.